Most Unexpected News

"The most appalling thing has happened," Tina put her head between her hands. "It's just too ghastly and incredible."

"Something has happened to Constance?" I guessed.

"What? Oh, you heard, did you? She's dead."

"Oh, my Lord? No wonder you're knocked out. When? And how?"

"I'm not really sure. Madam was pretty nearly hysterical. She kept yapping on about suicide. I couldn't understand it."

"Not just hysterical, off her head, I should say. Much more likely to have been a heart attack. Poor old Connie."

"Poor old Connie?" Tina repeated on a screeching note. "My God, Tessa, I do believe you think I'm talking about Mrs. Bland."

"Who else?"

"Constance McGrath, that's who else. You know. She's the girl they call Hattie."

Bantam Books offers the finest in classic and modern English murder mysteries. Ask your bookseller for the books you have missed.

MURDER IN OUTLINE

•

Anne Morice

BANTAM BOOKS

TORONTO • NEW YORK • LONDON • SYDNEY • AUCKLAND

MURDER IN OUTLINE

*A Bantam Book / published by arrangement with
St. Martin's Press, Inc.*

PRINTING HISTORY
St. Martin's edition published August 1979
Bantam edition / February 1986

ISBN 0-553-25647-5

Published simultaneously in the United States and Canada

*Bantam Books are published by Bantam Books, Inc. Its
trademark, consisting of the words "Bantam Books" and the
portrayal of a rooster, is Registered in U.S. Patent and
Trademark Office and in other countries. Marca Registrada.
Bantam Books, Inc., 666 Fifth Avenue, New York, New York
10103.*

PRINTED IN THE UNITED STATES OF AMERICA

H   0 9 8 7 6 5 4 3 2 1

MURDER
IN OUTLINE

ONE

"So I am invited to be a judge," I said, putting the letter down. "How gratifying! And it must show that I am beginning to make my mark on the world. You agree, Toby?"

This was during one of my rest periods, part of which I had been spending with my cousin Toby at his house at Roakes Common. My husband, Robin, who is a Detective Inspector at Scotland Yard, had joined us there on Saturday evening, bringing a bundle of mail from London, including the invitation just referred to.

"Much depends on what you will be judging," Toby replied. "If it is the vegetable marrows at the Storhampton Agricultural Show, I dare say the mark will not be indelible."

"Oh no, something much grander. They want me to be on the panel of judges at the annual inter-house competition of the Waterside Drama and Ballet School. How about that?"

"Isn't that your own *alma mater?*" Robin asked.

"One of them. I spent two years there. My parents settled for it when I was clamouring to leave school and go into pantomime. Waterside was a compromise because they do teach a few other things as well, like history and grammar and all that."

"We'll take your word for it," Toby said.

"It was lovely too," I went on, ignoring this. "Easily my favourite school. Probably even better than panto, in a way. Madam was rather a pill though," I added reminiscently. "Always carrying on a deathly feud with poor Miss Lawrie, who was very meek and no match for her."

"Madam who?"

"I can't remember her name. She was head of the arts

1

side and only ever known as Madam. Miss Lawrie was her opposite number, in the scholastic department, and she was nicknamed Annie, need I tell you? I have an idea she's retired now, but she never impinged very much on my life. My highest ambition at the age of fourteen was to become a ballerina at Covent Garden, but Madam said I was too tall and too turned in and that every one of my toes was the wrong length. That's when I switched to acting."

"And when does this competition take place?" Robin asked.

"26th to 28th June," I replied, having consulted the letter again. "It's a weekend, so I'll probably be able to fit it in, even if, God willing, I am working again by then."

"A whole weekend? A fair old marathon, by the sound of it."

"Well, no, not exactly. What happens is that on the first day they have the ballet sessions, which are not in my sphere, although I am invited to attend, more or less as a matter of courtesy. Then on Saturday, which is my bit, each house puts on a one-act play, or scene from something or other. They can write their own, if they want to, and they have to produce it themselves, as well as paint the scenery and make all the costumes. Each performance lasts about half an hour."

"And how many houses in this school?" Toby asked in an awed voice.

"Five," I replied, after a brief pause, to deprive him of the satisfaction of catching me counting on my fingers. "Red, Blue, Green, Brown and Orange, the last being mine. We wore orange armbands on our leotards and we were looked after by the dearest old matron-cum-housekeeper called Mrs. Patterson, known to one and all as Patsy, in case you hadn't already guessed."

"And what happens on Sunday?" Robin asked, his training and experience once again prompting him to dig out the hard facts.

"Oh, that's Speech Day, when the two winning performances are given all over again for the parents and governors. There's also an Art Exhibition, so called, and one or two of the more respectable exercise books are propped up for inspection, just to reassure everyone. Of course, I'd have been invited to the Sunday fling, anyway, being an old girl. I've only been to it once, as it happens, and that was the year when I got my first job and wanted to show off a bit; but I shall certainly be there this time. You can come too, if you like."

Robin managed to conceal any feelings of ecstasy arising from this suggestion and Toby said:

"I can't help feeling that time has drawn a somewhat spangled veil over this brief period of your life. Can it all have been quite so halcyon as you now make out? Was there not the occasional sticky patch?"

"Oh, indeed! I've already mentioned the running battle between Madam and Annie Lawrie, but neither of them was half so alarming as our terrible, awe-inspiring principal, Connie Bland, trumpeting about and putting the fear of God into one and all; especially that ghastly day when Amanda Blake was caught smoking after lights out. It is an experience I never wish to live through again."

"You mean it was all right to smoke, so long as the lights were on?"

"No, of course not; I was simply trying to recall some of the rough, as well as the smooth, of those far-off days. There was Dr. Bland, for instance, Connie's husband and business partner. Not that there was anything bad about him, quite the reverse, in fact, but he had a rather exciting reputation in the extra-marital field. And there was a grown-up daughter called Pauline, who had to be carted away one night in an ambulance. It was given out that she'd got acute appendicitis and she reappeared about a week later, looking wonderfully pale and wan, but Tina Blundell said she knew for a fact that Pauline had taken an overdose and we all believed her. So, you see, it wasn't all beer and skittles. Still, you know how it is at that age? One fastens on anything which relieves the monotony and life wouldn't have been half so much fun without its moments of drama and tragedy."

"Strange how radically one alters in maturity," Robin remarked pensively.

TWO

(1)

Waterside School was situated midway between Goring and Oxford, three miles from the small market town of Gillsford and so named because of its position on the banks of the Thames. Indeed, there were periods during most winters, when the river swelled up and overflowed into the meadow on the opposite bank, when one had a strong sensation of living actually on the water, instead of merely beside it. In summer, however, the benefits were reaped, for no lawns were ever greener, no flower beds more brilliant with colour, and no prouder woman in the land than our formidable, success-worshipping principal, Mrs. Constance Bland.

The main building, a long, low and imposing white pile, had been constructed to his own specifications by a local Victorian businessman, in the grounds of a much older house which had been partially burnt down and then left to decay. Fortunately for posterity, he had chosen a style which belonged somewhere in between these two periods, thus achieving the best of both worlds: solid Victorian construction, combined with elegant Regency design. Furthermore, he had had the prescience to site it not on the main river, which nowadays would have been intolerably noisy in summer, but on a private and parallel stretch of backwater.

The only part of the original still intact was the stable block, with its blue-faced clock tower and enclosed brick quadrangle. Or, rather, the façade remained intact, most of the interior having recently been converted into a modern, well-equipped theatre.

Dr. and Mrs. Bland had been owners of this property for some dozen years, having acquired it in the following manner:

After scouring the country in vain for a suitable school for their daughter and only child, Pauline, Mrs. Bland had eventually solved the problem, with typical daring and panache, by founding one of her own. Pauline, at the age of nine, had been declared by her teachers, inspired less perhaps by impartial judgement than the desire to find favour with Mrs. Bland, to possess a natural gift for music and dancing, in addition to a quick mind and studious nature. Accepting this verdict without surprise, it had occurred to Mrs. Bland that the first requisite was a school which would foster these various talents in equal degrees. This might conceivably have been attainable had she not also demanded, in her refusal to accept second best in any department, that the surroundings, both inside and out, should conform to the highest standards of taste and comfort.

Since, so far as painstaking investigation could evince, no such establishment existed, she had instantly set about creating it, this venture having its origins in the medium-sized Queen Anne town house in the centre of Gillsford, which Dr. Bland had inherited from his father, along with a flourishing medical practice, and which was then the family home. A resident governess had been engaged, plus a regular supply of visiting teachers in the specialist subjects, and a small advertisement placed in *The Times*.

Mrs. Bland had received scores of replies to this, mainly from parents in a similar plight to her own. Having interviewed all those with engraved addresses which struck the right note, the applicants had been whittled down to five girls between the ages of nine and twelve and, a month later, the Constance Bland Preparatory School, as it was then known, had come into being.

This, as with every other venture she touched, had been a roaring success and in only three years the move had been made to Waterside House, the number of pupils increased to forty and the age limit extended to seventeen.

Dr. Bland still retained the ground floor of the old house for his surgery and consulting rooms, but the remainder had been converted into flats, the school in the meantime rising to such dizzy heights that a few years before I joined its ranks Mrs. Bland had extended the premises still further by acquiring the next-door property. This was called The Lodge and, although aesthetically inferior, was almost equal in size to Waterside and she was able to double her numbers yet again.

Sadly enough, the only drop-out in this heady, steady climb to success was the one for whose sake it had come about. After all the early promise, Pauline's talent seemed to have waned in adolescence and fizzled out completely by the time she was old enough to leave school. To the best of my knowledge, the only two distinctions she had achieved there were the Divinity prize and her Girl Guides Life Saving badge.

Mrs. Bland showed no regrets about this. She was not one to waste time or sympathy on failures and Pauline, after all, had served her purpose. She was packed off to spend six unhappy months with a family in a Paris suburb and afterwards had worked for a time with her father's medical team, answering the telephone and sending out bills and suchlike, but with such pathetic inefficiency that the rest of the staff had eventually demanded her dismissal. Pauline had returned to Waterside to become general dogsbody to her mother and a buffer state between headquarters and the teaching staff, a boring little niche which, now in her mid-thirties, she still occupied.

Headquarters, which is to say the private apartments of Dr. and Mrs. Bland, consisted of half a dozen of the larger and more attractive rooms, including a semicircular collonaded veranda overlooking the garden, and access for the pupils was strictly by invitation only. This could take one of two forms, the more common being to receive a reprimand so grave that the threat of expulsion hovered in the air throughout the interview, although judgement was usually tempered by mercy for those with very grand or rich parents. The other was when a group of more presentable-looking seniors was granted the privilege of handing round the apéritifs at one of Mrs. Bland's cocktail parties.

On this occasion, owing to my exalted twin position of Judge and Old Girl, I had been invited to spend Friday to Sunday at headquarters, but the rosy glow which Toby had remarked on did not quite extend to memories of Connie Bland and I had quailed at the prospect of spending three whole days under her shrewd and critical eye. So I had explained that Robin was hoping to accompany me to at least part of the festivities, which was not a perfectly accurate way of describing it, and that we had therefore arranged to spend the weekend with my cousin Toby at Roakes Common, about twenty miles away.

However, there was one event in Friday's programme which, from sheer curiosity, I had decided to attend. This was scheduled for four-thirty in the afternoon, when tea would be served to visitors and staff in the music room.

Anxious not to be late, I had allowed extra time for all sorts of contingencies on the drive from London, none of which actually occurred, and, as a result, turned into the Waterside drive at least twenty minutes too early.

There were only two cars parked near the front door, one of them being easily identifiable as the property of Dr. Bland. He had always driven a white Rover and he had regularly exchanged it for a new model every summer, very likely during the same week as he ordered his annual supply of wine and cigars. The second car was a shabby old Volkswagen which, assuming she too had remained true to form, could only have belonged to Pauline.

Equally reluctant to be the first as the last to arrive and aware that Mrs. Bland would frown quite as heavily on such pushing behaviour as on unpunctuality, I parked my car at a distance of about fifty yards from the house, in the protective shadow of the wall which separated the drive from the kitchen garden and stable block, and remained seated inside it for a few minutes, fixing my eyes hungrily on the rear mirror for signs of other guests arriving.

It was a case of the watched pot, however, and, as it happened, the only action came from a point some distance ahead of me, when three girls came tripping out of the

quadrangle and made their way halfway down the length of
the house to the front door. They were all wearing long
black cloaks over their blue and white print dresses and
they were giggling and chatting as they strolled along,
displaying to perfection that unselfconscious grace which
seems to get built into every dancer, however youthful and
inexperienced. It was clear from their relaxed and cheerful
demeanour that they had not been summoned to headquarters with the threat of expulsion hanging over them, so
presumably were to be members of, or more likely waitresses
at, the tea party. This at least carried the assurance that I
had come on the right day, as to which certain doubts had
begun to creep in, but it also acted as a warning that the
present lull might be deceptive and that I was in imminent
danger of being caught red-handed in my skulking operation and, worse still, forcibly rescued from it. So I decided
to use up the remaining time by embarking on a sentimental pilgrimage to some of the old haunts.

(2)

Directly ahead of me and at the opposite end of the house
to the veranda, was a covered brick path, dividing the
kitchen premises from the stable yard. It led to the river
bank and a set of stone steps down to the towpath and a
boathouse, just visible through overhanging trees, and I
had an urge to see this boathouse again. It had been the
focal point of some of the happiest hours I had spent at
Waterside, for it had housed, among other and grander
craft, two elderly punts, and during the summer term about
a dozen of us at a time had been allowed to take them out
on our own for an hour or two in the late afternoon.

Punting was forbidden, on the grounds of being too
dangerous for such feckless and inexpert crews, but there
were half a dozen paddles to each punt and on the rare
occasions when we had all pulled together we had managed
to work up quite a decent speed on the downstream trip to
Gillsford Bridge.

The exercise was enjoyable, not only in itself and in the sense of freedom it gave, but also because it was one of the very few outdoor activities permitted to us. Team games and riding were strictly banned, since they tended to develop the wrong muscles in a dancer's anatomy, and the only sports we were encouraged to take up were tennis and swimming. However, as there were only two tennis courts at our disposal, no swimming pool at all, and the river too polluted for safety or pleasure, our chances of indulging in these recreations were somewhat limited.

It cannot be claimed that anyone who spends a minimum of one hour's daily practice at the bar is seriously deprived of physical exercise, but nevertheless we frequently compared our lot unfavourably with our contemporaries in other walks of life and the fact was that, whereas most private schools raise money from bequests, endowment funds, parent blackmail and all the rest of it, to provide just those amenities which were lacking at Waterside, Mrs. Bland had decreed that every last penny that could be scraped together in this way should go towards building and equipping the theatre. This policy resulted, I had always suspected, less from her passionate dedication to the arts as from the belief that the shows which were mounted there were distinctly more palatable to parents, prospective parents and influential visitors than the sight of numerous muscular females flopping in and out of the water, while the rest of the school stood on the sidelines and screamed.

I did not meet a soul on my way down to the river, but seated at the top of the flight of steps and hunched over a sketch pad was a stout female aged about sixteen. Her blue and white dress was crumpled and paint-stained and the already dusty black cloak had been rolled up to make a cushion. Nevertheless, I was immediately drawn to her by virtue of the orange headband round her untidy brown hair and bade her a civil good afternoon. If she had been Claudius at prayer, she could not have started more guiltily.

"Sorry," I explained, "I didn't mean to scare you to death. It was the sight of another human being which made me bark like that."

"Please don't apologise," she replied, scrambling to her feet in a surprisingly clumsy and unco-ordinated fashion. "It's only because I'm not supposed to be here at all that I almost had a heart attack."

"Mind if I join you for a while?" I enquired. "I have an urge to feast my eyes on the boathouse. I'm Theresa Crichton, by the way."

"And you're one of the judges. I know, I recognised you. Waterside's pride and joy! Patsy always lets us stay up to watch television when you're on, however late it is."

"Good for her! What's your name?"

"Actually, it's Constance McGrath, but you can't have two Connies in the place, so I've come to be known as Hattie. I expect you can work that one out, being an Old Watersider?"

"I thought he was Mad Dan McGrew?" I asked, after a pause for mental convolutions.

"Near enough."

Although so ungainly in her movements, there was no gaucheness of manner and in the course of these introductions she had slid into the Walter Raleigh role and was spreading out her cloak, so that it covered almost the entire flight of steps. Graciously motioning me to the top one, she re-seated herself a few steps lower down, placing the sketch pad behind her and out of sight. She then produced a tin of butterscotch, offering one to me before going to work on them herself.

"The reason for all that surprise at seeing you here," I explained, "was that the whole place seems so unnaturally deserted. If I didn't know it for a fact, I would never believe that there are up to a hundred people going about their business behind these walls."

"You wouldn't say that if you'd been anywhere near The Lodge. It's absolute bedlam. Three dress rehearsals, one after another, and everyone screaming that they've forgotten their lines and their costumes don't fit. Patsy's so busy taking tucks and trying to calm everyone down that she won't notice whether I'm there or not; and Connie's got her tea party to keep her occupied, so it was a good chance to skip away for a bit of peace and quiet."

"You amaze me! Things must have got a lot more lax since my day. As I recall, every single one of us, not exluding the halt and infirm, had to pitch in on these occasions, even if it was only as third spear carrier or helping with the make-up. Unless, of course . . . you wouldn't be in the ballet group, by any chance?"

"You must be joking! I was five foot ten and twice as wide before I was fourteen. Madam kicked me out years ago. And they know so well that if they ever did give me a spear I'd only trip over it. No, I designed the set and that's my lot. They can all prance about on it to their hearts' content, so long as they don't expect me to join in."

"Then, forgive me saying so, Hattie, but isn't it all rather a waste of time?"

"What is?"

"Your being here at all. I mean, the education's not all that hot and if you don't want to dance and you don't want to act, what's the point of staying on?"

"Oh, plenty of point, believe me! It's not this dump that's the attraction, it's the fact that they let me go for two whole days every week to art classes at Oxford. There and back in a taxi too, for which no doubt my father has to cough up about four times the fare; but I ask you, what other school would let you do that? 'Oh no, dear', they'd say, 'First get your A levels and then you can make up your mind what you want to do.' That's no use to me. I decided ages ago what I wanted to do and A levels don't come into it. I don't know how many A levels David Hockney has. Four dozen, I dare say, but I bet he'd have been just as good a painter with none."

"I expect you're right. Is your father coming on Sunday for Speech Day?"

"No, he's in South America. He's an ambassador. It makes a nice change after his last posting, but it's a bit far off. And my mother's dead, so she can't be here either. Which means that I've got to be farmed out at some boarding establishment or other and I'd settle for this one any old day. You can say what you like about Connie; I know she's a snob and a tyrant and blazingly unfair sometimes, but she does understand about giving people a chance to develop in their own way. There's probably self-interest at work there too, but it happens to operate in my favour. I expect I shall quite miss her."

"Miss her? Why do you say that? She's not giving up, is she?"

"Not as far as I know. That'd be the day, wouldn't it? No, I meant that I'd miss her when I leave here at the end of this term and start at a full-time art school, that's all. It's coming up to four-thirty, by the way. You'll miss her yourself, if you don't watch it."

"Yes, I know," I agreed, curiosity about this unusually outspoken girl making me reluctant to leave, "but before I go won't you show me what you were working on when I interrupted you?"

"What? Oh no, you don't want to see that, do you? It's nothing in particular. Just a crazy idea I'm trying out. I haven't got it nearly right yet."

For the first time she sounded faintly ill-at-ease and on the defensive, signifying perhaps that this was something close to her heart and so when she eventually was persuaded to hand over the sketch I cautioned myself to be tactful and to take my time before giving an opinion. This was just as well because time was certainly what it needed.

In contrast to the smudgy little drawing of the boathouse I had been expecting, with possibly a few fuzzy willows in the background to lend perspective, this was a precise and delicate pen-and-ink drawing, crammed with detail and executed with immense care and exactitude. And that was not all. There was a touch of the Blake about it, not to mention the Bosch and, even more than admiration of the technique, it was wonder at the mind which had conceived it which temporarily rendered me speechless.

In essence, it was a picture of birds, beasts and fish, not connected with each other in any recognisable way and with no attempt at realistic proportions, a particularly repellent-looking hyena, for example, being about four times the size of the lion. Some were in full face, others in profile and every single one, however tiny, had the face of a human being. One or two were easy to identify, as much by behavioural characteristics as by their features. The plump and smiling dolphin in the centre of the picture, for instance, puffing a cigar and holding a glass of wine in one flipper instantly brought Dr. Bland to mind and surely the squirrel in the bottom left-hand corner could only be Patsy, her little pile of nuts representing the secret caches of toffees and chocolates which were always brought out for those in trouble, most particularly the poor little homesick new girls who lay sobbing in their beds at night.

There were others, though, that I could not place at all, among them the lithe, long-legged cat halfway up a ladder, which seemed to be perched on the dolphin's back, and the scruffy-looking bird, with its bow and arrows, the arrows, for some reason I was quite unable to fathom, being bottle-shaped.

Although, on her own admission, it was still unfinished, the theme of this work was left in no doubt, for it already bore the stark, somewhat alarming title of "Schizo".

I did not think it would be fitting to ask for any amplification of this and, indeed, was at a loss for a suitable comment of any sort, except to say that I hoped to see more of her work when there was time to study it carefully.

Hattie did not reply, but held out her hand for the drawing, with an enigmatic expression, and when I turned back to wave goodbye to her she was bent cver her sketch pad again, apparently once more oblivious of my existence.

THREE

The three graceful girls were on duty in the music room and one of them bobbed a plate of cucumber sandwiches under my nose, while dropping the regulation Waterside curtsey.

"I'm dying for one," I told her, "but I'll be in trouble if I don't say how do you do to Mrs. Bland first."

"She's not here. Vanished."

"Really? Where to?"

"No one seems to know. It was a case of 'now you see her, now you don't'. Rumours are circulating, but nothing official. Perhaps she forgot to go before she came. Pauline's doing the honours."

This, as I now saw, was true. She was presiding at the lace-covered table, with a huge silver teapot wobbling about in her hand and looking as though she might lose her grip on it and everything else at any moment. However, there was nothing unusual about this and it did not betoken anything seriously amiss. I had never greatly cared for Pauline and furthermore I knew I should get no information from her because she was notoriously unobservant and no one, least of all her mother, ever told her anything.

So I held my ground and snatched a cup of tea from a passing tray. When I turned round again I found that the cucumber girl had moved on and that her place had been taken by another, although unfortunately she had not brought anything to eat. This one, in fact, was about the same age as myself and at first I thought that, like most of the other twenty or so guests, she was a stranger to me. However, as soon as I heard: "Hallo, Tessa!" in that deep, husky and somehow reproachful voice, it all came back. Her name was Tina Blundell and for almost a whole term she and I had been best friends. Soon afterwards she had been gathered into Madam's small circle of favourite protégées, this coinciding with the time when I was pronounced to be the lowest of all the duds, and thereafter our paths had moved along parallel lines, only now seeming, when viewed from a distance, to have joined at any point.

She had been orphaned at birth, as I now recalled, and of unknown parentage, which worried her dreadfully, a state of affairs for which her adoptive parents had done little to compensate. They resented her, we were led to believe, not only for growing up to be shy and plain and for preferring dancing classes to the Pony Club, but for the still more illogical reason that she had survived, while their only natural child, a boy some years older, had been drowned in a boating accident soon after his eighteenth birthday.

She had changed considerably in appearance since then and her hair was now drawn severely back and parted down the middle, in traditional ballerina style. Also the years, or possibly skilful make-up, had helped to fill out the long, narrow face and enlarge her eyes; but she still possessed the same extraordinary legs, which seemed to start from just below her ribs, and she still looked as fragile as cigarette smoke, although I happened to know that she had the stamina of twenty camels.

"Teeny!" I chanted, much overjoyed. "How marvellous to see you! Does this mean you're a judge too? Oh, I am glad!"

"Not on your life; and do you mind not calling me Teeny? Or, at any rate, not shrieking it aloud all over the room? I happen to be staff."

"You are? Oh, I see," I said, badly deflated.

"You needn't sound so sorry for me. I always wanted to teach, you know."

"Yes, I do remember your saying that, but I thought it was only because you had a slight crush on Madam and wanted to follow in those hallowed footsteps. And with all your terrific talent and dedication . . . well, I mean, it seems such a waste somehow. If anyone looked set for a blazing career it was you."

"Yes, that's what they all said, so I felt obliged to give it a try. I went straight into a ballet company in Milan when I left here. Stayed with them for nearly three years, in fact."

"But it didn't work out?"

"Oh, from a career point of view it was getting better all the time. And they were nice people too, some of them. But it simply didn't suit me. I was absolutely rigid with fright whenever I had a solo part; literally sick with nerves for hours beforehand."

"Well, I bet most people are."

"Yes, I know, but most people also get that lovely glow when they've brought it off. That must make up for everything, I suppose, but it never came my way. I just haven't got the temperament for the big time. I'd have been all right if I could have stayed in the corps, but where's the future in that? I decided I'd be better off teaching."

"Yes," I admitted. "If I throw a great effort into it, I can appreciate that, but you didn't have to come back to a potty little place like this, did you? Surely, with all your qualifications you could have got taken on by one of the really grand schools? I don't see how you can bear to be shut up in old Waterside all over again."

"It's not a potty little place and I'm not shut up in it all over again. I have a very swanky flat in Gillsford. I teach here three days a week, for which I'm paid slightly more than the going rate, and the rest of the time I can give private classes, or do what I damn well please. Besides, every dancer has to start somewhere and you ought to know how important it is for them to have expert tuition in the early stages. We get a few brilliant ones, even here, from time to time. There's one at the moment, as it happens, only unfortunately. . . ."

"Unfortunately what?"

"Oh, never mind. It's a long story and not a particularly pleasant one. Besides, you're not here to discuss the life and hard times of Tina Blundell. You'd better go and do your stuff with your fellow judges. They've got that radio announcer whose sister was at school here in the dark ages and the other one is . . ."

"Yes, all right, but just hang on for a moment because there are a couple of things I simply must ask you."

"You haven't changed much, have you, Tessa?"

"No, and neither have you; but for a start, who's the stunning, feline creature in the pale blue suit?"

"Would you be referring to Madam?"

"No, I would certainly not be referring to Madam. This one is all of fifty years younger. Look, she's gone into a huddle with Pauline now. She was talking to Billy Bland before that, but now he seems to have vanished too."

Tina looked across at the tea table, then broke into one of her deep throaty laughs:

"That just proves how long it is since you bothered to come to Old Girls' Day, or even open one of the Waterside news letters. That's Madam all right. The old one, who taught you and me, died three years ago."

"Oh really? What of? I mean, I realise she was terribly ancient, but somehow I always expected her to live forever."

"I never heard the details. I was abroad when it happened. Perhaps it was not having poor Annie Lawrie to fight with which finally undid her. I dare say she pined away from sheer frustration. What else did you want to know?"

"What's become of our hostess? It's unlike Connie to leave the stage halfway through the scene and I can't really believe that she would forget to go before she came, so what's the answer?"

"Right here," Tina said. "She has just re-entered. In fact, they both have; Billy in attendance."

At this point the girl with the cucumber sandwiches bounced up again, apologising for her desertion and for the fact that there were now only two left. I took them both and she said:

"Oh, goody! That lets me off the hook. I can now mingle unencumbered. All is revealed, by the way. Someone overheard Madam giving out the news to Pauline. Connie had a spasm of some kind and was forced to retire and send for her very own doctor."

"What sort of a spasm, do you suppose?" I asked Tina, when our informant had tripped away on her mingling spree.

She gave another of her rather eerie laughs, which sounded a bit like the last of the bathwater gurgling down the plughole.

"I see you haven't outgrown your passion for minding other people's business, have you, Tessa? Do you remember how cross poor old Annie used to get because you would hold up the lesson with your endless questions?"

"Yes, and I still can't understand why it made her so ratty. I thought the whole purpose of education was to foster the enquiring mind."

"Except that so few of your questions had any relevance to the subject she was trying to cram into us. And, if you ask me, the only kind of spasm Connie would be likely to suffer from is a spasm of rage. It was probably just a ruse to get Billy out of the room, so that she could tick him off."

This remark reminded me of another reason for my friendship with Tina coming to such an abrupt and painless end. Her brains, as Miss Lawrie had been apt to remark, might all be in her feet, but it was chastening to remember how often her feet had been right.

"And this is Theresa Crichton, one of our star pupils," Connie announced, introducing me to the radio announcer. "She had her name up in lights in Shaftesbury Avenue three months after she left us."

This, needless to say, was the wildest exaggeration, but all her pupils had quickly become accustomed to acting as pawns in the game of advancing the glory of Constance Bland and it would not have occurred to me to trim her statement down to something a little nearer the truth, even if I had not, for the first time in my life, found myself feeling a little sorry for her. She genuinely did look groggy and there was a misted, apprehensive look in her normally alert brown eyes. I looked forward to another encounter with Tina and the pleasure of telling her that this time she had got it wrong, for if further proof were needed that this particular spasm was not due to spleen, it was provided by the fact that only illness could have made her forget that I had met this broadcaster innumerable times before.

His name was Eddie Harper and he had been around for a good many years. Tall, upright and military in bearing, he was the very opposite of that in manners and personality, which were invariably humorous and easy-going, taking setbacks lightheartedly, and trivialities with pretended seriousness. In fact, I often thought he had modelled himself on a Wodehouse character, languid and slangy and appearing much more obtuse than was often the case. On the whole, I approved of this, for if you cannot have the real thing in Wodehouse characters, and life does seem to decree that you can't, then a pale imitation may be the next best thing.

Unfortunately, however, he had departed from the original in one very important feature, which was in marrying each of the girls he had become engaged to. There had been three previous wives and the current one, whom I was now hauled over to meet, was called Vera and she was about half his age.

She had other attractions as well, including a massive supply of dark hair, liberally streaked with autumn tints, enormous dark eyes and a noble profile. Her figure was on the dumpy side, however, and she had also been cursed with a mournful expression and whiny voice, suggesting that deep down there was a sombre side to Eddie's character, or else that he was inclined to marry women he felt sorry for.

Far and away the most enduring love of his life was Waterside School, possibly because of the number and variety of females under its roof. He visited it at least twice a year, either to judge a competition or to present prizes and, on more than one occasion, had stepped into the breach, when some other lecturer dropped out, to give us a talk or, rather, string of anecdotes entitled "Early Days of Broadcasting", and consisting largely of jokes against himself. As a result, in my day at any rate, he had been held in great affection by the girls and we had passed many happy hours debating whether, assuming them both to be forty years younger, we should have chosen to marry him or Billy Bland.

Evidently, sentiments had not changed very much in half a generation. The party was now beginning to break up and I noticed while I was talking to him that the three pretty waitresses had bunched themselves into a group and were hovering with some impatience in the background. So I gave them the floor and instantly two of them grabbed him by the arms and invited him to take a turn outdoors, on the pretext of wishing to show him their hamsters, or something equally feeble.

Eddie responded with alacrity, pausing only to remind me that I had promised to take a jugful of dry martini with him and Vera at their hotel as soon as the sun went over the yardarm, before carefully placing his feet, right heel to left instep, in the number two position, in preparation for setting forth.

Vera, however, who, although within earshot, had not been included in the invitation, now intervened, saying plaintively:

"But you won't be too long, please, Eddie? I find I have one of those wretched headaches coming on. I should go back to the hotel and lie down, if I am to be any use to you all tomorrow."

Eddie smiled at each of the girls in turn, then withdrew his arms from theirs and turned round:

"Right away, old love. Hang it, why didn't you murmur something before? Farewell, then, my proud beauties! I shall see you all in the morning."

If Toby had been present, I should have opened a book with him. Two to one against that marriage lasting the course.

Tina trotted up again as I was getting into the car.

"You're not playing truant, by any chance?" she asked.

"No, back tomorrow morning. Ten-thirty on the dot."

"But I thought you'd been invited to stay?"

"I was, but I wriggled out. I was afraid a whole weekend with Connie would be too much for me. I'm staying with my cousin Toby who, as you'll remember, lives at Roakes Common. It's about twenty miles away, which is a bore, but better than commuting from London."

Tina frowned, which is something she should never have done, her eyes being set quite close enough together as it was.

"If I'd known that, I could have invited you to stay with me. That's only three miles away."

"Has it got the telephone laid on?"

"Of course it has, you ass. It's Gillsford, not the Sahara."

"And is the invitation still open?"

"But you just told me. . . ."

"I know, but that's no problem. I'll ring Toby up and explain. I don't expect he'll cry himself to sleep over it."

She dug into her bag and produced a ring with two keys on it. Holding one of them up, she said:

"Okay, fine! This one is for the main door, which isn't locked until after six o'clock. The other is for my flat and I've got a spare. Do you mind going ahead on your own? I've got to take a rehearsal in a minute. It may be a couple of hours before I'm through and I'm sure you won't want to hang around. Top floor and your room is the one with the yellow chintz curtains. Help yourself to whatever you want."

"Thanks awfully, Tina, you are an angel! But listen, what's the address and how will I find it?"

She stared at me as though I was demented and then gave out the plughole laugh:

"Didn't I explain? You won't have any bother finding it. It's the Blands' old house. You know, where Billy carries on his surgery, among various other less medical practices."

FOUR

(1)

Having confirmed that Toby was indeed in no danger of crying himself to sleep, I next put a call through to Robin to inform him of the change of plans. He was not in his office, so I left a message asking him to call me back on Tina's number after eight p.m. All this took some time, mainly because I was reversing the charges, so during the intervals, as I waited for the operator to sort it out, I had the opportunity for a thorough inspection of my surroundings, and very impressive I found them.

As Tina had mentioned, the flat comprised the top storey of this elegant, early eighteenth-century house and had clearly been intended for attics. It had dormer windows let into the roof and those sloping ceilings which always lend charm and character to a room. All of which I had been prepared for, but the unexpected feature was the style in which it had been fitted out. The curtains, carpets and wallpaper all looked expensive and new, there was a great air of comfort throughout and every room contained at least one rare and beautiful object, none of this being in any way associated with my memories of Tina, who in childhood had always been indifferent to the creature comforts. It puzzled me until I realised that it must be all the work of Connie Bland. Probably the salary just about covered the rent and hence the need for private pupils.

Having concluded my business, I left a note in the hall, in case Tina should return before me, and set off on foot along the High Street to the Nag's Head Hotel, where the Harpers were staying.

Eddie was on his own in the ferociously oak-beamed and dimly lit bar, slumped on a stool and staring moodily into an empty glass. This did not alarm me, however, because, like many people whose conversation was spattered with jokes and ribaldries, his face often looked melancholy in repose.

"Ah, there we are, my dear old adjudicator! I was beginning to fear you had stood me up. Two more of the same, please, barman!

"Let us wander over to a table," he went on when this order had been dealt with, "so that we can converse in undertones and plan how to rig the judging tomorrow."

"That reminds me, Eddie: I was told there were to be three of us. Who's the third?"

"I am, of course."

"No, you're not. You're the first and I'm the second. Who else?"

"When you put it like that, I am bound to say that the answer is Vera."

I regretted that he felt bound to say this because, as well as finding Vera rather a drag, I suspected that her presence on the panel might seriously interfere with my own arrangements. Not that I had the slightest intention of rigging anything at all, but it had certainly been my hope that Orange would excel themselves and that Eddie and I would speak with one voice in declaring them the runaway winners. Something warned me that Vera was unlikely to be so co-operative and, furthermore, I could not imagine how she could qualify for the job anyway.

Fearful that some of these misgivings might have been betrayed by my wooden expression, I hastened to say:

"Oh, that's nice! How's the migraine, by the way?"

"Pursuing its deadly course, I'm afraid. Flat on her back, with the curtains drawn, poor girl. She sent you a thousand apologies, but she didn't feel well enough to come down."

"I'm so sorry. Does she often get these attacks?"

"Too often for comfort."

"All her life?"

"I gather not. Just the past few years. And kindly don't rush to the conclusion that it was being married to me that brought them on. I agree that it would be enough to give anyone a touch of the migraine, but in this case I think it's banging her head against the jolly old Iron Curtain which has caused the damage."

"What does she want to do that for? Okay, Eddie, I've already been ticked off once today for asking too many questions, so you're at liberty to shut me up if I'm being tactless."

"My dear old judge, as though you could! Nothing tackless about it. If Vera could be with us, she'd be delighted to tell you herself. Though it's just as well she isn't, I might add. Her English isn't steaming hot at the best of times and she's apt to get worked up about those geezers on the other side. Unfortunately for her, she was born in the wrong place, with the wrong name and the wrong-shaped nose, to mention only three."

"Oh, how rotten! Still, at least she managed to get out?"

"Eventually, she got as far as Israel, which wasn't quite far enough, as it turned out. She was on her own, which is a situation she finds hard to cope with, being one of life's clinging vines, and she couldn't get work there either."

"What sort of work?"

"Thespian. Treading the b. Whatever it's called nowadays. Barnstorming is probably the word I'm looking for."

"You never told me she was an actress, Eddie."

"Did I not? It must be my innate respectability which makes me shun such words. Or possibly I'm getting senile. You'll soon learn to take it in your stride. Anyway, we met when I was out there, doing a documentary about co-operative grapefruit or something. I went to the theatre in Tel-Aviv one evening and there, looking very natty with her tray of ice creams, was Vera. Love at first sight. Fortunately, I happened to be wifeless at the time, so happy endings all round. And time for another drink, by the look of things."

He did not give the slightest hint of having married Vera principally in order to provide her with a British passport, but I dare say senility was to blame for this omission too.

"So she's all right now?" I asked, when he had returned with fresh supplies from the bar.

"Well, if you can call cooking and scrubbing for an old codger like me being all right, yes, I suppose she is. And she's found some faith healer or guru, or some such rascal, who operates from the Cromwell Road. She swears he's doing her migraine good, but I doubt if the nasty thing will go right away until she gets some better news about her family. We're working on that, but I doubt if I'll be alive to see the day. And how are you, love of my life? Pecker up? Mustn't grumble?"

"No, I mustn't grumble."

"Splendid! And what about that copper you turned me down for? Robin something or other. Know the one I mean?"

"Yes, and he mustn't grumble either. I'll tell you one who might legitimately grumble though, and that's Connie Bland."

"Ah! Pecker definitely on the dip, you'd say?"

"Didn't you notice how groggy she was looking?"

"I did, and the phenomenal thing was the speed with which it hit her. There she was, laying down the law and telling us all how wrong we were, just like her merry old self, and the next minute wham; her eyes were starting out of her head and she looked as though she had bitten into a live frog."

I was momentarily diverted by this description which brought a teasing memory of Hattie's picture. I was almost certain there had been a frog or a toad among her weird collection and I now began to plague myself by trying to attach a face to it. It was no use though and I returned my attention to Eddie, who now wore the hurt expression of one who had just made a joke and watched it sink like a stone.

"Sorry, Eddie, I was wandering. What did you say?"

"At your age! No, never mind, and the fact is that one shouldn't be flip about it because it strikes me that dear old Con could be for the high jump. Must be almost as old as I am, after all."

"No, you'll always be young. And what makes you think it's so serious?"

"Something Billy let fall. He asked me how I thought she was looking and I said: 'Oh, fit as a fiddle' and all the rest of it, as one does on these occasions, at which he hung his head and muttered grave words. I got the impression he was worried."

"So presumably this wasn't the first time she's had one of these turns? It raises an interesting question, doesn't it, though, Eddie?"

"If you say so, old girl, you being the arch-priestess when it comes to the raising of interesting questions."

"Is a practising physician allowed to treat his own wife?"

"The interesting answer comes down heavily in the negative. I am sure it would be frowned upon by the B.M.A. His name would be mud, if not worse. In theory, that is. I dare say some chatty enquiries re the headache and indigestion are tossed to and fro across the breakfast table. Irresistible, wouldn't you say? Like being married to a plumber and not being able to call on him to give a hand with changing the washer. I dare say even that chap Robin comes to the aid of the party from time to time. I expect if you were honest you'd admit that was your only reason for marrying him instead of me."

"Because he's so good at changing the washers?"

"Come off it, dear old fathead! I refer to a whisper that has come to my ears about your running a sideline these days in the amateur detective business. True?"

"If you say so, Eddie. Who whispered it?"

"Oh, I still get around in one or two high places, you know, even on these creaking old pins. Is it true?"

"Sort of, but for goodness' sake don't say a word to Connie. I am sure she wouldn't regard it as at all a suitable occupation for one of her ex-pupils. Anyway, all this talk of Robin has reminded me that I'm expecting a call from him, so I must hurry away and station myself by the telephone. Thanks for the drink and I'll see you tomorrow."

"Ten-thirty sharp, as ever will be."

"Oh, and give Vera my love and say how sorry I am."

"I'll do that, my angel, but she'll be as fit as a flea in the morning and all set to take her place beside us on the bench, don't you worry."

"Oh, good!" I said, that being the last thing I was worried about.

The lights were on in the attics of Queen Anne House, as it was so appropriately named, indicating that Tina had returned earlier than expected. There were also some chinks of light on the ground floor, but a thick wedge of black in the middle of this sandwich, the first and second floors evidently being currently unoccupied.

As I walked up the short path from the gate on to the High Street, where the white Rover was parked, I saw a woman letting herself out by the front door in a somewhat stealthy manner and closing it silently behind her, and I concluded that she was a late patient. So many of Billy's late patients were women and stealth was their middle name. Nor was I knocked out with astonishment, on coming face to face with this one under the porch lamp, to find that she had the round, staring, slightly inimical eyes of a cat.

"Sorry, but the surgery's closed now," she said in a distinctly hostile voice.

"No matter, I have my own keys," I informed her.

"Excuse me, but you must be mistaken. This is private property. You've obviously come to the wrong house. If you tell me who you're looking for I may be able to help you."

"I am looking for my friend, Tina Blundell," I said, bringing out the keyring with a flourish and then pivoting round her to unlock the front door. "And I don't need any help at all, thanks all the same."

"And cats have claws," I reminded myself, as I plodded up the three flights of stairs to the top flat.

(2)

"So if I'm not to call you Teeny any more," I said, digging into the sausage and scrambled egg which she had been cooking when I let myself into the flat, "what am I supposed to call you? Not Miss Blundell, by any chance?"

"You can call me anything you damn well please, just so long as you don't go bawling it out in front of the girls."

"I bet they call you Teeny behind your back."

"I bet they do too, and worse things than that, no doubt. The point is that I find it hard enough to maintain my authority as it is, without having you at my elbow to undermine it still further. Besides, it's the kind of thing which infuriates Madam. She can't abide what she calls these silly, affected pet names."

"Ha! Bit bolshy, is she?"

"You could put it like that, I suppose, but who cares? The important thing is that she knows her job backwards, forwards and sideways, and if she is able to inject a little dose of democracy into out maternal dictatorship, well, so much the better is what I say."

"Although I don't imagine Connie Bland has much trouble keeping her in her place?"

"It comes naturally with her. She was born with the iron hand in the spiked glove. Is that your only question for this evening?"

"By no means. I have a whole string of them lined up for you."

"Like what, for instance?"

"Like, let us say, for instance, how long has this thing been going on with your democratic Madam and your paternal dictator, Billy Bland? What's her real name, by the way?"

"That's two questions."

"Take them in whichever order you prefer."

"Her name is Janet Haynes."

"And?"

For a moment I thought Tina was going to come the innocent, but after a slight pause she said:

"I'm afraid I can't tell you how long it's been going on. Unlike you, it usually takes me more than a couple of hours to unravel these secrets."

"But you have known about it for some time?"

"A month or two, I suppose. They've taken to meeting downstairs in the surgery just recently; ever since the flat below this one became vacant, in fact. The first floor is used as offices and showroom by an interior decorator, so that's always safe outside business hours."

"And is it now common knowledge? Bandied about in the dormitories and so forth?"

"I wouldn't have said so. On the whole, they're fairly discreet. It's just that living here means that I've had it rather forced on my attention. Even so, I doubt if I'd have caught on if I hadn't run into her in the hall one evening and, instead of behaving normally, she lost her head and spun some yarn about having run out of sleeping pills, as though it was necessary to give an excuse for being there. Since then I have to confess that I've been slightly more alert."

"Do you suppose Connie knows?"

"Couldn't tell you. Sometimes I think Connie only knows what it suits her to know."

"I call that a most profound observation, Teeny, and well worthy of you. The fact is, it might suit her very well to know all about this and to turn a blind eye."

"Why might it?"

"Because her eyes may be small, but they're very wide open and I doubt if she nursed any illusions about being pretty or attractive, even in her youth. On the other hand, innumerable women have found the dear doctor ravishingly pretty and attractive. Realising what an old philanderer he was, she may well have decided that the only way to hang on to him was to let it ride. Like most easy-going people, he's not the type to suffer rows and nagging gladly and so, stuck with that situation, it could obviously suit her better to have him philandering with one of her own employees, where she could keep an eye on things and, if necessary, apply the occasional brake. So how's that for an analysis of life in the Bland boudoir?"

"Quite good. I had come to roughly the same conclusion myself."

"And Janet is not married, I take it?"

"Divorced. She and her husband used to be joint owners of some ballet school in London. It was when they split up that she took the job here."

"Why here, I wonder?"

"Why not?"

"Oh, come on, Teeny! Feet like yours can soon work that one out."

"I'm not sure I can be bothered to. Do you want the last sausage?"

"Why don't we share it?"

"Well, we seem to have thrashed out that subject pretty thoroughly," I went on, when she had completed the delicate operation on the sausage, "so let's move on to the next one. Tell me about Hattie?"

This time there was no gurgle of laughter and she put her fork down and regarded me with a mixture of amazement and displeasure.

"Honestly, Tessa, you really take the bun, I have to admit it. You arrived here this afternoon at what time was it? Half past four? And already you've uncovered enough to be curious about Hattie. What's the secret?"

"I arrived at ten past four, as it happens and, funnily enough, that's the secret. Explain, though: what's Hecuba to Hattie?"

"I'm not sure I can. She's quite an enigma, our Hat. A compulsive eater and grossly overweight, for a start. Two things which wouldn't normally be tolerated at Waterside, and Madam practically has apoplexy if her name is mentioned. It's not as though she were particularly bright either. She was bludgeoned into taking three O levels last year and she didn't get so much as a pass-mark in one of them. And yet, and yet . . ."

"She does have other talents?"

"So you know about that too, do you? I might have guessed! Well, it's true that her drawings are rather clever and original. Some of them were accepted for the County Exhibition and she won a special award, which sent her soaring even higher in Connie's estimation, but I still wouldn't have thought it warranted all the special privileges she gets."

"I gather her father is a biggish wig?"

"And stinking rich with it. I dare say that's the whole boring answer; and yet sometimes I feel there must be more to it than that. If it wasn't so patently absurd, you could almost believe that she had some kind of hold over Connie. She really gets away with murder, that girl."

"Last question coming up," I said, as we sloshed our way through the washing up. "This afternoon at the tea party you said something about having a rather brilliant student this year, but there was a sad story attached to it. What was all that about?"

"Proving that no stray remark is too stray for you to train your microscope on? Actually, it's the reverse side of the Hattie coin, the girl who can do no right. So far as Connie is concerned, that is. She's called Belinda Jameson and simply bursting with talent. I'm not sure she'll ever make it as a classical dancer, but she's a marvellous all-rounder. Good singing voice too. Only sixteen, but in the opinion of myself and various other people too numerous to name she has real star quality. And she works like a demon, what's more. I've often caught her plugging away, on her own, in the studio long after the practice session was officially over. One more year here and she'd be all set to go right to the top."

"No heartbreaks in this story, so far."

"No, but here's where they start. She won't get the chance of one more year. She leaves at the end of this term."

"Moving on to higher things?"

"On the contrary; moving on to the scrap heap. She's being chucked out because she can no longer afford the fees. Her father's business went bust a couple of years ago and he shot himself."

"How rotten! And you mean Connie demands her pound of flesh, even in circumstances like that and even though she's got such a winner on her hands? That surprises me. I know she's ruthless, but she's canny too and I'd have thought this girl would have been a good enough advertisement to make it worth while keeping her on free of charge."

"So would I, so would anyone in their senses, but Connie loses hers when it comes to hard cash. And furthermore the father was self-made, from one of the lower social drawers, which makes Belinda doubly guilty in her eyes."

"You'd better get hold of her home address and let me have it some time."

"What for?"

"Believe it or not, Teeny, I do have a few strings to pull in certain quarters and there may be some auditions coming up."

"Oh I see! Well, personally, I think she'd do far better to stay on here and finish her training, but if you think you can help, I suppose a job wouldn't be such a bad alternative. Thanks."

"I can at least try. How did you hear about all this?"

"Belinda told me herself. She's miserable about it, poor child. Sees her whole career going down the drain before it's even begun. I also happen to know that Madam tried to intercede for her. Suggested they could get round the problem by everyone chipping in to set up some kind of scholarship, but Connie wouldn't even listen. Quite apart from the monstrous imhumanity, the sickening waste of it maddens me. Honestly, one feels like throttling that woman sometimes," Tina said, swilling out the washing-up bowl with great gusto and grimness. "And now, Tessa, I hope that really was your last question. I don't know about you, but personally I'm whacked and I have to clock in at eight-thirty to-morrow morning."

She was right, as usual, and hardly finished speaking before I became engulfed in yawns. Two minutes after climbing into bed I fell asleep and at some point during the subsequent eight hours had a most prophetic dream. I was floating along past row after row of disembodied faces, some beautiful, others hideous and deformed. There was no sound, but they were all mouthing at me and after a while I found myself able to lip read. Every one of them was repeating over and over again:

"Constance is dead, Constance is dead."

FIVE

There were two entrances to the Waterside auditorium. The official one was by way of the foyer, which opened off the central stable block, and at right angles to this was another set of externally identical buildings which had been converted into garages and now housed the art exhibition. The unofficial way was through one of the sliding glass doors which covered the theatre's entire length on its right-hand side and which were approached from the gardens of The Lodge. Black curtains were pulled across these doors during performances, but at other times they were left open, to enable the audience to stroll about outside.

I chose the second means of entry, having arrived half an hour early, purposely to pay a call on Patsy, which I felt to be already overdue.

This being Saturday, there were no schoolroom classes and I found her ensconced in her cosy, cluttered little sitting room, looking exactly as I remembered her best, one dachshund on her lap, another draped across her feet and half a dozen of the most recent intake of juniors seated in a semi-circle on the floor, while she read aloud to them from her own favourite book, *The Wind in the Willows*.

She looked up at me over the top of her reading glasses, when I had knocked and been bidden to enter, and then, when the hugging was over, and I had been introduced to one and all, she put aside the book, brought out a box of peppermints from her secret hoard and proceeded to regale us all with tales of my dashing exploits as a schoolgirl. They were largely apocryphal, but the little girls were not yet of an age to carry a pinch of salt in their mental equipment and lapped up every word. It was quite a wrench to tear myself away from the happy scene, and Patsy also appeared to feel that something had been left unfinished. She walked to the head of the staircase with me, saying:

"Come back and see me again, my duck, if you get a moment. Such a lot I want to hear."

"I certainly will, but there's nothing wrong, is there, Patsy? You look a bit worried. Don't tell me you've found a toffee pilferer in the Lower Third?"

For a moment she looked quite aghast, then recovered herself and laughed in an embarrassed kind of way:

"Same old Tessie," she said, patting my cheek. "Always such a tease!"

There were three minutes to go before Curtain-Up on the first play, and a senior girl, no doubt acting as Front of the House Manager for the occasion, was standing by, ready to black out the windows. She signalled to one of her minions, who were dotted about at various points in the auditorium, to show me to my seat and provide me with the tools of my trade. These consisted of a programme, writing pad, ball-point and several marking sheets.

I was sorry, although not particularly surprised, to find that Vera had fulfilled the promise made on her behalf and turned up. Not in a very cheerful mood, however, by the look of her, and she was wearing a singularly unbecoming black headscarf, pulled well forward over her forehead, which made her look more lugubrious than ever. I also had to concede that she looked far from well and I was struck by the depressing thought that practically every adult I had so far encountered at Waterside had appeared either anxious or ill, or, in some cases, both.

She and Eddie were seated in the centre of what was now the front row, the first four having been removed to make room for a table, which was tastefully set out with water carafes, crystal glasses and a large bowl of roses, in true Constance Bland style. My tactful escort guided me past this to a seat on Eddie's left, and immediately afterwards the lights dimmed and the curtain rose on three females in Edwardian dress, griping on about the tedium of it all and the desirability of getting to Moscow.

This was Green's offering and was to be followed by a half hour interval. After that our morning schedule required us to see two more performances, separated by another interval, the first of these being Orange's entry. The full programme was timed to end at twelve-thirty, at which hour we were invited to luncheon at headquarters, to be followed by a conducted tour of the art exhibition. We should then see the two remaining plays, bringing us to four-thirty and the end of the day's stint.

It was bad luck for Green that they should have selected a play by Chekov, for they could not have foreseen when the choice was made that one of their judges could claim to have appeared in it herself, in the original version and in a Russian theatre. Inevitably, Vera had nothing but contempt for their poor effort and I saw that I should not have to waste a moment talking her out of awarding them a high score.

Indeed, she went to the opposite extreme and announced, loudly enough to be heard on stage, as well as by a group of partisan spectators up in the circle, that they deserved no more than three marks out of a possible ten in each section, Design, Direction and Acting. So I evened the score up a bit by giving them a total of twenty-five, which was at least five more than they deserved, and then suggested that we spend the remainder of the interval sunning ourselves on the terrace.

I suspected Vera of being about to refuse, on principle, but fortunately Eddie was all in favour and had stood up and offered her his arm before she could formulate her objections. With head down and clutching the knot of her headscarf in the manner of one who had been invited to take a stroll on the Siberian Steppes, she allowed herself to be led outside.

The flagged terrace which separated this side of the theatre from the lawns and flowerbeds surrounding The Lodge, was set out with pretty bamboo furniture and, with masterly timing, as we emerged on to it a girl came across the grass, carrying a tray of coffee and biscuits.

"You have to hand it to the dear old gorgon," Eddie remarked, as I poured out. "She may not be in the pink of health, but she has not lost her touch."

"Yes, it's almost daunting, isn't it, how well the wheels are oiled? Of course, she's been able to profit by yesterday's experience with the dance sessions. Any little hitches that occurred then will have been ironed out for our benefit. I forgot to ask who won that, by the way. You don't happen to know?"

"Green, I think," he replied, "or it might have been Blue. Brown, perhaps? I get so confused by all these complicated names."

"Never mind," I said, "because here comes one of my acquaintances who can almost certainly put us straight on it."

The reference was to Hattie, one of the group of girls who had been watching from the circle and who were now wandering out on to the terrace. She was carrying a sketch pad and a bulging sackcloth bag.

"Brown," she answered promptly, when the question had been put to her. "Everyone knew they would and they did. Five of them are in Teeny's class, so it was a foregone conclusion."

She then proceeded to explain that she had been granted the special privilege of sitting in at every performance, having been commissioned by Mrs. Bland to make a pictorial record of the entire event.

"Sort of official war artist," she added, eyeing the plate of biscuits in a speculative fashion. This did not pass unnoticed by Eddie, who pushed it in her direction and urged her to fill her pockets, a suggestion which, somewhat to my amazement, she obeyed almost literally, scooping up

a handful and popping them into her sack, before saunter-
ing off in search of pastures new.

The three unhappy Russians were followed by five miserable London girls, sharing a flat in Fulham, in an excerpt
from a play I had recently seen in London. On the face of
it, this was a sensible choice, but in fact the inexperience
and immaturity of the cast showed up much more glaringly
in a contemporary setting and even by stretching loyalty to
the limit I could award them no higher marks than had
been earned by their predecessors.

The final performance of the morning, however, was
on a totally different level, and far outshone the others. It
was a one-acter, specially written for the occasion, about a
vaudeville troupe at the seaside and included a number of
song and dance turns, to the accompaniment of an on-stage
piano. The device, as we all agreed, was unoriginal, but it
was hard to fault the production and even Vera grudgingly
admitted to being impressed by the brilliance of the star
performer, whose name, the programme informed us, was
Belinda Jameson.

In view of her present and impending troubles, as
related by Tina, no one could fail to admire the spirit and
discipline as well at the artistry she displayed.

Janet Haynes, alias Madam, came in person to escort
us to headquarters for lunch. So absorbed were we in the
tour de force on stage that none of us had noticed her come
in, but when the curtains were drawn back and sunlight
flooded in again I was that she was sitting at the end of the
row and applauding as enthusiastically as the rest of us.

Our brief consultation concluded, and resulting in an
aggregate of eighty-six marks, which effectively put paid to
Orange's chances, Madam moved up a few places and
introduced herself.

Evidently, she had done pretty well out of her share of
the London ballet school, for on this occasion she was
wearing a cream-coloured dress and jacket, with plenty of
pearls and a heavy gold bracelet. She was in a conciliatory
mood too, and thanked us very graciously for consenting to

be shut up in a stuffy theatre on such a glorious morning. Eddie gallantly responded by saying that he would cheerfully endure such incarceration for a week, if he could be guaranteed such ripping entertainment, but Vera threw one of her spanners into these happy works by complaining, as we passed through the foyer, that it had indeed been insufferably hot and, since this had caused unbearable discomfort to her feet, she would be obliged to change into another pair of shoes, which she had left in the car.

Eddie promptly offered to scuttle off and fetch them for her, but as she rather churlishly pointed out, this would only have resulted in her wearing one pair and his carrying the other. So we parted company and Madam and I were left to battle on alone in finding pleasant things to say to each other, as we covered the remaining hundred yards to the house.

It was not until we were on the last lap of all that she managed to dredge up a form of apology for her rudeness the previous evening; whereupon I assured her in one breath that I had not noticed it and had also understood the reason for it. However, instead of leaving it there, she launched into a stream of explanations about having made a special journey to the surgery to collect a prescription, only to find it closed. This giving rise to such transports of frustration and annoyance as to make her careless of what she was saying and whom she was saying it to. All the same, she did not offer any explanation for the surgery lights being switched on and the doctor's car parked outside, and nor did I bother to enquire how she came to possess her own key. I was wondering whether she genuinely so underrated my intelligence, or whether she was going out of her way to leave no misunderstanding whatever concerning her relationship with Billy Bland.

In any case, I considered that she was taking on a formidable opponent in the person of Connie, for the hand on the Waterside helm had by no means lost its strength, as was demonstrated once again when we reached the front door and a girl came panting up the steps behind us. She was carrying my jacket, which I had left on the terrace during one of the intervals and forgotten to reclaim.

It was only days later, when I was doing some total recall about missing change from a ten-pound note, which I had used to pay for petrol, that it struck me that it had been in the pocket of this very jacket.

SIX

(1)

The guests were received in the hall, which was spacious enough to serve as an all-purpose sitting room. It had an Adam-style fireplace at each end and a curved double staircase going up through the centre to the gallery above. All this grandeur, needless to say, was off limits to the girls, who shared a side entrance and linoleum-covered back staircase with the domestic staff.

Connie Bland was standing by the fireplace on the right of the front door, talking to an elderly and wizened man, wearing a tweed knickerbocker suit, who looked like a gamekeeper or poacher. He even had his spaniel, alert and motionless, by his left boot, and I judged him to be either a very exceptional man or else the owner of a very exceptional dog, as in general these animals were anathema to Connie, being arch-destroyers of Persian rugs and polished floors.

The answer, as I discovered by degrees, was a bit of both. It undeniably was a model dog, sitting, standing and prostrating itself at a single, staccato word of command from Master, but then, on the other hand, Master was no ordinary man either. He was a retired doctor, who had been in partnership with Billy's father and had recently added to this distinction by inheriting a vast fortune from a widowed sister in South Africa.

It was a relief to find Connie once more her old stately, implacable self. The anxious, vulnerable look had gone and sure proof that she was back on form came when, in the space of two minutes, she informed me that she might be old-fashioned, but personally she considered it bad taste to wear eye-shadow in the daytime, that there was such a thing as being too thin and that those shoes looked dreadfully uncomfortable for walking in. Having fired these broadsides, she walked away in search of a fresh victim, leaving it to Dr. Birkett to pick up and reassemble my shattered morale.

However, this mention of shoes had reminded me that Eddie and Vera were certainly taking their time in retrieving hers, so I asked the doctor/poacher a question about his dog, which I hoped was guaranteed to take him some minutes to answer and, while he did so, was able to devote half my attention to watching for the Harpers' return.

After about ten minutes, when the dissertation on the pedigree, intelligence and loyalty of Smudge, such being the creature's undistinguished name, appeared to be running out of steam, I noticed that Connie was also becoming restive and had twice glanced from her watch to the front door.

A few seconds later Eddie came hurtling through it. He was on his own, flushed and harassed-looking and with *sang* most untypically *chaud*. He muttered a few words to his hostess, which I was too far off to hear, but fortunately I was seated next to him in the dining room and, without any prompting at all, he gave me a full run-down on the situation.

It appeared that the story of the shoes had merely been an excuse. The truth was that Vera's migraine had returned in full force and she had needed, above all, to get away quietly on her own for a while, to down a few pills in private.

Eddie, meanwhile, had regained his self-possession and when I asked why Vera could not simply have explained all this, instead of making a mystery of it, he grinned and said that, hard as I might find it to believe, she was one of those stoics who would consider it bad form to make a fuss if she were being dragged to the stake. Also, he added, she hated people getting the idea that she was the sort of neurotic woman who lived entirely on pills. Since, in my opinion, she probably was the sort of neurotic woman who lived entirely on pills, I found this understandable.

"So she's gone back to the hotel, presumably?" I asked. "Was she really fit to drive there on her own?"

"Not on your nelly. Not now or ever."

"Really? You mean she doesn't drive at all?"

"Never managed the test, for which I bless those stout-hearted fellows who had the job of putting her through it. Vera beind the wheel is a concept one rather shrinks from. I was all for delivering her at the hotel myself, but she would have none of it. Said it would make me late for the beanfeast and upset the whole schedule, thereby bringing Connie's wrath down on both our heads. All perfectly true, of course, but rather beside the point. However, no talking her out of it. Like so many of these stoics and martyrs, she has the strongly developed mulish streak. So anyway, here I am, sitting next to the most beautiful girl in the world, which goes to show that silver linings are definitely on the increase."

"Thank you, Eddie; but, to get back to Vera, where did she go?"

"Nowhere. She's sweating it out in the car, poor old love. I implored her on my knees to come indoors and suffer in comfort on some Regency chaise longue, with which this house no doubt abounds, but I gather that sort of thing comes into the category of making a fuss."

"But she can't spend the whole afternoon in the car, surely?"

"Not on your life. She intends to be fighting fit in a couple of hours, when the jolly old pills have got to work. Nothing would induce her to miss the judging, I must tell you. Having put her hand to this plough, she will plough on till sunset."

I had hoped to hear more, but Dr. Bland was seated on my other side, at the head of the table, and I could sense his affectionate, mockingly reproachful brown eyes fixed upon me. Aware that I had committed no end of solecisms by neglecting him for so long, I swung my head to the right

and flung out a few enquiries relating to the cause and effect
of migraine. The replies were interesting too, providing
much food for thought. This made it an extra-special
occasion for the records because the food, in the material
sense, was also on a most superior level. Coquilles St.
Jacques, with Chablis, had now given way to fillet of beef
and a sidelong squint at the labels on the claret bottles,
which were to accompany it, gave ample cause for awe and
wonder. It made me realise that I had spent two whole years
at Waterside, eating up my Irish stew and prunes like a good
girl, without ever having the slightest conception of the
gourmet orgies which must have been taking place only the
width of a wall away. It just proved how true that saying is
about one half knowing so little of the other, even when
both halves are living under the same roof.

Dr. Bland had altered a little since those days,
although some of the changes, I suspected, were not
entirely due to the passage of time. His hair had gone from
streaky grey to purest white, but it was still thick, and curly
at the ends, and his complexion was still bronzed to a deep
tan. He had always given the impression of having recently
spent three months climbing up a mountain or lying on a
Caribbean beach and, since it was indisputable that he had
never done either of these things, we had been inclined to
attribute the sunburnt look to a dash of oriental or possibly
Red Indian blood in his ancestry. This, naturally, had
added considerably to his appeal, although I believe his
principal attraction lay in his eyes. They were very dark
brown and usually brimming with mirth and kindliness,
which I felt sure accurately reflected his character, for
although he was a great tease, I had never heard him utter
an unkind word to anyone.

These qualities had remained undimmed too, as he
proved, once the subject of migraine was out of the way, by
complimenting me on a recent television play and asking
some pertinent questions concerning the technicalities of
the production. We were still deep in this absorbing topic
while the plates were being cleared away and replaced by
clean ones for the next course, and it may have been this

combination of circumstances which delayed my reaction to a slight commotion at the other end of the table. The first intimation came when I realised that Dr. Bland was no longer listening to me, but was looking straight ahead of him. I turned my head in the same direction and saw that Mrs. Bland had slumped forward over the table, apparently unconscious. A second later Billy rose from his seat and moved round the table towards her, with Pauline, after a moment's fluttering indecision, following suit; but it was Dr. Birkett who reached her first. Placing one hand on her wrist and the other on her shoulder, he gently pulled her back into her chair. Whereupon she opened her eyes, slightly shook her head and stared at us in an affronted way, as though we had played some stupid trick on her.

"What's the matter? What are you doing?" she asked in a slurred but still aggressive voice.

"Not to worry, my dear, you'll be all right in a moment," her husband said, having now taken a firm grip on her left shoulder. "You turned a little faint for a moment, that's all; so just come along upstairs and we'll soon have you right again."

She seemed about to protest, but then I saw the frightened, vulnerable look return to her eyes and, with a faintly despairing gesture, she allowed the two doctors to haul her to her feet. Billy waved Pauline back to her place at the table and the three of them made a slow and staggering exit to the hall. At which point a horrid silence fell over the whole party, followed by an outburst of inane chatter.

This was brought to an end by Billy re-entering the room and announcing that the time had come for Pauline to escort the judges to a preview of the art exhibition. Docile as ever, she sprang up, flashing her toothy smile and all but clapping her hands in childlike glee:

"Ooh, lovely idea! Lucky me! Shall we go?"

Muttering our awkward and nervous goodbyes to our host, Eddie and I also obediently rose to our feet and followed Pauline out of the room.

(2)

There were several cars on the circular gravel space outside
the front door, but none so far as I could see with a solitary
occupant.

"Which is yours?" I asked Eddie.

"Further down, under the trees near the gate," he
replied. "She'd have felt a bit conspicuous up here. Didn't
much care for the idea of every Carol, Jane and Emma
popping their heads in the window to ask if she wanted a
glass of water."

For the first time I felt a touch of sympathy for Vera,
having been prompted by similar inhibitions to make the
excursion to the boathouse, which had led to my encounter
with Hattie.

"Sorry about that unfortunate mishap," Pauline said
with a high-pitched giggle, when Eddie had sauntered off in
search of his wife, and she clasped my arm in hers and
pressed herself close up against me.

I resented both word and deed, for I always feel
uncomfortable in close physical contact with someone I
dislike and the principle reason for disliking the otherwise
inoffensive Pauline was her propensity to the kind of
remark she had just uttered.

Even as a child, I had dimly perceived how cowed and
frustrated a creature she was and how humiliating her
position, both at home and in school, but such sympathy as
this had engendered had been eaten away by her irritating
habit of trying to ingratiate herself with us girls, particularly
the elder ones, always pretending that she was secretly in
our camp and then scurrying off to spread tales to her
mother, in order to curry favour in that quarter.

I had additional cause to dislike her now because of
her facile assumption that I was still the same immature,
sniggering idiot who would find something intoxicatingly
funny in the spectacle of an elderly autocrat being brought
down by illness.

"It must be a great worry for you," I said primly.

"Oh, it is, you've no idea," she agreed vehemently, quickly changing the tune, as was her habit when snubbed. "And the worst of it is she's so obstinate. Simply won't admit there's a single thing wrong with her."

"Has it been going on for some time then?"

"Several months, anyway. I can't exactly remember when she had her first attack. Round about Christmas, I think."

"And your father hasn't been able to diagnose it?"

"Oh yes, I think he knows, poor Daddy, but what can he do, if she . . . ?"

Pauline was obliged to break off at this point because we had reached the entrance to the art exhibition and someone came blundering out of it and nearly knocked us flat. It was Vera and she appeared to be in a bad way.

"Where is Eddie?" she asked in a faint voice, ignoring our expressions of pained astonishment. "I must find him, please, this minute. My head is so bad. I should go back to the hotel."

"He has gone to look for you," I told her. "He thinks you are in the car."

"No, no, I could not stay there, it was too hot. I think I must get some air. Then I met someone who told me where the exhibition was being held, so I thought I would be able to sit down somewhere more comfortable. But it is such a long wait and my head feels like bursting. So now I must find Eddie and ask him to drive me home."

"Here he is now," I said, as he came marching briskly through the archway towards us. "Your troubles are nearly over."

"Aha!" he called, giving us a wide salute. "So I was right, wasn't I? Guessed she'd be here and here she jolly well is. And how are we feeling now, old duck? On the mend, are we? Well no, it doesn't look as though we are," he continued on a sadder note. "Better face it, I suppose, you're feeling rotten? Come along then, we'll go back to the hotel and you can put your feet up. How's that?"

"But only if you promise to return," Vera said, sounding quite vigorous all of a sudden. "You are simply to take me as far as the door and then turn round and come back. Is it understood? I cannot bear you to let all these good people down; these girls who have worked so hard and who love you so much. You will do as I ask?"

"Whatever you say, old lady," Eddie assured her, looking somewhat embarrassed by this impassioned and plucky appeal. "And, having got that lot off your chest, how about bowing out and putting the best foot forward?"

"I ask your forgiveness," Vera said, now addressing her noble sentiments to Pauline and myself, "but my wretched illness shall not inconvenience anyone for more than just a short while."

"The only snag is," Pauline muttered, watching the Harpers' slow, laborious progress to the archway, "even if he does get back in time, it will still leave us with one judge short."

The same drawback had occurred to me and I waited to see how she would deal with it. The outcome was predictable.

"Listen, Tessa," she gabbled, "could you be a saint and go and look at the pictures on your own? You'll find one of the sixth form on duty inside, who'll tell you anything you want to know, and I really think I ought to dash off and have a word with Mummy about this crisis."

"Okay, Pauline, but I suppose you do realise that your mother may not be in any state to cope with the problem at the moment?"

"She'll be in a far worse state if we try to sort it out on our own," Pauline said as she scuttled away, and I had to concede that it was one of the few pertinent remarks I had ever heard her utter.

Hattie was on reception duty, seated behind a trestle table. Alongside the inevitable box of sweets, which she stopped bothering to conceal when she saw it was only me, were some roneo-ed sheets of foolscap, serving as catalogues, and a Visitors' Book, which I was invited to sign. There were already half a dozen signatures for that day, the first three being those of the Bland family, followed by J. K. Birkett, then Janet Haynes and last of all Vera.

"Did she do the rounds?" I asked, pointing to this one.

"It was cursory," Hattie admitted. "I think she was making a stern effort to be dutiful, but found it a strain. She came out after a couple of minutes and we had a bit of a chat. Then we heard you and Pauline coming and she went flying out, saying she had to get some air."

"She suffers from migraine."

"I know, she told me; and also how she'd had to miss lunch and everything, as to which I could personally sympathise, having got wind of the menu. Was it as good as it sounded?"

"Every bit. What else did she talk about?"

"Nothing much. She wasn't here very long. In fact, I'm afraid I did most of the talking. I thought it might cheer her up to know that she had a fellow sufferer from one of the blights of this life, so I told her what a ghastly bore it was being so fat and how I kept on eating, because I felt depressed about it, which made me fatter than ever. You know, the good old syndrome?"

"And did it cheer her up?"

"Seemed to. She became quite animated for a minute or two. Said she'd suffered from exactly the same when she was about my age, couldn't keep her hands off the chocolate and cream buns, but there was nothing to worry about because, with a little help from one's friends, one more or less got over it. Something on those lines; and I must say I've heard it all before, no fewer than a million times, but I think she meant to be kind."

"Yes, well, that's a point in her favour," I said rather abstractedly, being less concerned now with Hattie's predicament than with the mystery of two people, so soon after the event, describing it in such very different terms. It was also something of a puzzle that an adolescent girl from an oppressed minority group in a Communist state should have found the wherewithal to stuff herself with cakes and sweets.

Predictably enough, Hattie's pictures far outshone

everything else on view and I was glad of my catalogue because she had worked in so many different styles that it would have been impossible for the uninitiated to attribute them all to the same artist.

There were a number of flower pictures, for instance, slapdash and bold and some quite ravishing in their colours; a few abstracts in patterns of brown and grey, which left me cold; and one huge, purely conventional portrait, dominating the entire room, of a stern, middle-aged man in full regalia of scarlet jacket, plumed hat and sword. There was a note in the catalogue to explain that this was the painting which had won a special award at the County Exhibition and I guessed that her father's pride in her achievement might be mitigated to some extent by the knowledge that numerous members of the public were now aware that, as well as a small mean mouth, he also had a slight squint.

The drawing of animals, birds and fish, with their human faces, was not on show, but there were one or two others in the same genre, including one of a masked woman, bound in chains, with what appeared to be a corpse at her feet, which had the depressing title: "Perils of Revenge"; and another, evidently completed too late to be listed in the catalogue, which was quite startling in its impudence.

It was a cartoon of three heads, placed one above the other and all instantly recognisable. The top one showed a female wearing a headscarf and peering through a miniature telescope; below that was a man with a rather asinine expression on his face and one eye opened much wider than the other, to accommodate his monocle. Underneath these there was a second female head, in profile like the first one and, in my opinion, a poorer likeness, with an enormous magnifying glass dangling in front of her nose. This drawing was captioned: "Judgement Day".

"Congratulations!" I said on my way out. "You've got us to the life."

"Oh, do you honestly think so? You are a marvel, Tessa! I'll give it to you, if you like? I'll have to take it down, anyway, before Connie starts bringing the nobs round tomorrow. I only put it in for a lark."

"Thanks very much. I'll hang it in my dressing room, where it is bound to excite much comment and admiration."

"Oh, terrific! Do you want to take it now?"

"No, I've got another session coming up in the theatre and it might get crushed in my bag. Give it to me tomorrow."

"Without fail," she said earnestly. "It's a promise."

Although one which, unfortunately and through no fault of her own, she was unable to fulfil.

SEVEN

The theatre was in semi-darkness, just one curtain partially drawn back, but even in the shadowy half-light there was no mistaking that stiff and resentful back and I realised that Dr. Birkett had been sent on as Vera's understudy and also that he was alone in the front row.

"What have you done with Patch?" I asked, moving into the seat beside him.

"Down there," he replied, pointing under the table. "Name's Smudge."

"Oh, so it is! I must say, she's beautifully behaved."

"Got to be, hasn't she? Get a whacking otherwise. Knows it too."

At this point a girl, presumably Alison Metcalfe: Stage Manager, appeared in front of the curtain to apologise for the delay and announce that they had been asked to hold up the proceedings for a few more minutes.

"Hope the feller comes soon," Dr. Birkett said in a disgusted voice. "One thing I can't stand is hanging about."

"Nor can I, but I know he'll do his best and in any case a few minutes probably means precisely that. The schedule would never be allowed to get seriously out of hand in this establishment."

"Well, if they do start without him, you'd better be prepared to take on three people's work. No use relying on me for this sort of caper. My old bitch down there probably knows as much about the game as I do."

"So it was very good of you to step into the breach."

"Good, my foot! Don't run away with the idea that I offered my services. Got pushed into it by Pauline and that one they call Madam."

"Oh, so it wasn't Mrs. Bland's idea?"

"No, she's still out of action, don't you see?"

"Is she seriously ill, in your opinion?" I asked, trying to make it sound more like a friendly enquiry than un-ethical probing. Not succeeding particularly well, however, for he replied in his gruff, offhand manner:

"Couldn't tell you. Not my patient."

"Whose patient is she, then?" I asked, risking another snub.

"Oh, one of the partners in Bill's firm, I dare say. That's usually the way it's done. Matter of form, really."

"In what way?"

"Well now, look here . . . Ah, here he comes! Now perhaps we can get on with it!"

For once in my life, I was sorry to see Eddie, who now came bounding down the aisle, begging our pardons, announcing to all within earshot that the revels could now commence and effectively putting a stop to all conversation. Two minutes later the curtain rose on a lot of black shawls and indeterminate north-country accents, and we were into *Love on the Dole*.

This and the offering which followed it, an excerpt from *What Every Woman Knows*, were both adequately staged and performed, but there were no fireworks and no one who came near Belinda Jameson's brilliance; and so, since Dr. Birkett was only too thankful to be guided by Eddie and me, the winner was never in doubt. It was past four-thirty before the verdict was reached and just the moment for a reviving cup of tea with Patsy.

* * * *

She had evidently been expecting me, or someone else who never turned up, for there were two cups on the tray and she did not boil the kettle until I arrived.

"Tell me something, Patsy," I said, when we had touched briefly on such matters as the house plays, her own and Robin's health and some recent highlights in my career, "why did you nearly faint dead away when I suggested that someone had been pilfering the toffees?"

"Did I do that, Tessie dear?"

"That's how it looked from where I was standing."

"And nothing much gets past you, as I know from bitter experience. Oh, might as well own up, I suppose! You did give me rather a shock, you see. The fact is, we have one of those unpleasant little kleptomania cases on our hands just now."

"So it was the literal truth?"

"In a way, yes. At any rate, that's how it began. Poor little Anna Parkes was crying her heart out because she'd failed the intermediary and I went to fetch some of my very special fudge to cheer her up."

"But the cupboard was bare?"

"Except for a boxful of shavings. I knew that wasn't right, even though I am getting old and silly. Besides, this was back at the beginning of term and I'd only just bought them a week before."

"Since when there've been repetitions?"

"Several, I'm sorry to say. I've had to take to locking things up now, which is not very nice. And it hasn't cured the trouble. Quite the reverse."

"You mean it's got worse?"

"Oh, much. Two or three weeks ago was when it began to be serious. The girls started coming to me to complain that personal things were missing; from their lockers and so on."

"What sort of things?"

"Trinkets, bits of jewellery. Some of it quite valuable, if you can believe what they say. Money too. Of course, it serves them right, in a way. They're supposed to hand all that sort of thing over to me at the beginning of term and I dole it out as I see fit; but we all know that not everyone sticks closely to the rules."

"Have you told Mrs. Bland?"

Although she never minded being called by her own nickname; Patsy disapproved of such *lèse-majesté* towards the Principal and, surmising that this ban applied just as rigorously to old girls, I was careful to observe it.

"Oh, good heavens no," she replied. "And I pray it won't come to that. It's hard enough to talk to her about anything these days. I'm hoping that we can just struggle through to the end of term and it will all fizzle out."

"But you must have taken some action, Patsy?"

"Indeed, I have. It's not my first experience of this kind of thing, you know, and I've learnt a few tricks in my time. A week ago I made them all give up their Saturday afternoon to tidy out their lockers and cupboards. A real old spring cleaning job. I told them I was sick to death of all this moaning about things being lost and as it was probably due to their own carelessness we'd have a good turn-out and see what came to light."

"And did the trick work?"

"Up to a point. One or two bits and pieces turned up in some unexpected places, but no cash, you may be sure. I'm afraid we're dealing with a clever monkey here. My guess is that she scattered just enough of the stolen bits around to prove my point. That's the trouble with these naughty people, you see. They get so cunning. It starts off in a harmless sort of way, helping themselves to sweets and biscuits and so on; well, that's just plain old greed of course, but they find they're getting away with it and it makes them more ambitious. They want to try for something a bit harder. In the end it becomes like a disease and they can't any longer control it."

"And you think you know who this joker is?"

"Oh yes," Patsy replied firmly. "Not much doubt about that."

"Then why not . . . ?"

"Have her on the carpet and get her to own up? I've

thought of it, but it wouldn't really do. She's leaving, anyway, at the end of this term and then, as I say, it will all die down. Besides, if I were to accuse her to her face, it would be sure to get to Mrs. Bland's ears and then the fat would be in the fire. We're treading on delicate ground with this one."

"But even so, Patsy, how could she be so unreasonable as not to back you up? I realise she's not well, but surely that's a purely physical thing? Do you mean she's going off her rocker or something?"

Patsy gave me a strange, speculative look, blinking at me over the top of her glasses, as she poured out my second cup:

"Well, dear, I suppose it would take you to put it into quite those words, but confidentially, in my candid opinion, you're not far off the mark. As you say, we all know she hasn't been well lately and that may cause her a lot of anxiety, poor woman, but the mental breakdown, if that's what you'd call it, started long before. More than a year ago, looking back on it."

"Honestly? I'm afraid I've been rather out of touch. What form does it take? Loss of memory, that kind of thing?"

"Oh, much more distressing than that. You know what grand ideas she's always had? And her way of trampling over everyone and disregarding their advice? Well, we all managed to put up with it, I suppose, because in the old days she did run things so efficiently and so often she turned out to be right. Not any more though, I'm sorry to say. Her judgement isn't nearly as sound as it used to be and, what's worse, she gets these fixations; pure prejudice, most of them, but nothing will shake her. And the extravagance is appalling. Strictly between ourselves, Tess, it worries me dreadfully sometimes. Having to sit by and see the money thrown away on madcap schemes and silly unnecessary luxuries. One can't help wondering where it will end. Things can't go on for ever at this rate though, that I do know."

"What do you mean by luxuries?"

"Anything and everything which adds to her own glory, to put it in a nutshell. Perhaps you didn't notice, not being a very frequent visitor, but the entire theatre has just been redecorated especially for this occasion. As though anyone cared! It's their girls they've come to see, not the new upholstery. She's had the old house in Gillsford entirely redone too, and what that cost is something I can't bring myself to tell you. The latest is that she's taken on an extra garden boy at twenty pounds a week, because Holden complained he couldn't any longer manage the lawns on his own. You'd think it was some millionaire's castle, instead of a girls' school."

"What do you suppose brought all this on?"

"Well, as I say, she's always had big ideas, but it seems to have gone beyond all sense and reason now. I'll give you an example. We had a burglary here not so long ago. A real, professional one, I mean. It was one night when she and the doctor were up in London and the thieves got in through the scullery window. Mind you, I'll always believe those foreign servants they've got now had something to do with it, because these villains must have known exactly what they were after and where to lay their hands on it; but do you think she would report it to the police? No, she would not."

"How strange! Did they take much?"

"Only some jewellry and cash; well, quite a lot really, about a hundred pounds, which she always keeps in her bedside drawer. And there's a silly idea, if you like! So she said no insurance company was going to compensate her for that and where was the sense of dragging the police in? It would only lead to a lot of publicity in the local rag, which would probably upset some of the parents and get the school a bad name."

"Something in that, I suppose?"

"Oh, I dare say, Tess, but it's the high-handed attitude I find so worrying and where's it going to end? She keeps putting the fees up every year, to try and keep pace, and that's a pity too, in my opinion. I know Madam isn't at all pleased about it either. It goes against all her principles that only the very rich girls should get the chance to come here. Besides, it's not practical in the long run, is it? She'll end by pricing herself out of the market, and then what an almighty crash there's going to be. It makes you weep to think of it."

"Well, cheer up, Patsy! You must be planning to retire one of these days. No one more sorry than me to see the old firm go bust, but at least you'll have nothing much to lose financially, if it does."

I offered this small consolation with some trepidation, for she had always been secretive about her age and, although I judged her to be now in her seventies, that was no guarantee against giving offence. I have noticed that the older people become the more sensitive they are apt to be on the subject of retirement.

To my relief, she took it calmly, although evidently not much cheered up either:

"If only that were true, my dear," she replied sadly, "but it's not quite as simple as that. I had always hoped to end my days here, in these two dear familiar rooms. I haven't much saved up, I'm afraid, but Dr. Bland promised me years ago that, so long as there was a Waterside, there'd always be a home for me. I know he meant it too, but how long will there be a Waterside, that's what I begin to wonder? And he's just as powerless as all the rest of us, poor fellow. Oh well, never mind, that's quite enough about my troubles. Tell me some of the theatre gossip. I'm so out of touch these days and you must have no end of excitement, now you're beginning to do so well."

I endeavoured to oblige, but soon resigned myself to the fact that she was only giving me half her attention, being irretrievably sunk, apparently, in her own doubts and worries, and when she had asked me the same totally irrelevant question for the third time I gave up the struggle, making the excuse that Tina was expecting me at the flat.

She looked older and sadder still when I said goodbye and I could not help wondering whether, despite all my present good intentions, I should ever see her again.

EIGHT

Tina was in the kitchen and a snarling rage, banging pots and pans about and with such a deep frown creasing her forehead that her face looked like a carving fork.

I started to bring her up to date with the results of the competition, but she only grunted and glared at me and so, in pursuit of my role as chief booster of the impaired morale of Waterside females, I said consolingly:

"Well, one good thing has come out of it, anyway, Teenie."

"Glad to hear it. What?"

"Connie will have to climb down now. She couldn't possibly sack that girl, Belinda, after the performance she gave this morning."

"Ha ha!"

"No ha ha about it. If she's even half as good at the gala show tomorrow all the governors and parents, not to mention the local press, will be falling about at her feet. If Connie has a grain of sense left, she'll be paying the girl's mother to allow her to stay on."

"Then it may interest you to know that she hasn't a grain of sense left. And it may also interest you to know that not a single governor or parent or member of the press will get the chance to see Belinda tomorrow. She is in solitary confinement and all they'll see is her understudy."

"Yes, I am very interested indeed. Has she got cholera or something?"

"No, she's been expelled. She is to be sent home tomorrow."

"You must be joking?"

Tina's grim expression showed plainly that this was not so and I pressed for details.

"Connie caught her stealing. At least, that's the story."

"Stealing what?"

"Literally dipping her fingers in the till."

"What till? I didn't know you had one."

"It's new since our day, but they've turned one of the downstairs rooms at The Lodge into a kind of shop. It's open for an hour every afternoon and the whole of Saturday morning and the girls can buy Coke and yoghourt and stuff like that."

"And?"

"Connie popped in there some time this afternoon, probably to make sure it was well stocked up with all the right vitamins and health foods when the parents came round. She claims to have found Belinda in there, at a time when she had no business to be, and that she was helping herself from the till."

"And what does the defence say?"

"Don't ask me! You don't imagine we live in a democracy up there, do you? Presumably, that she was putting in the exact money for the bar of chocolate she'd taken, or whatever; but what good would that have done her? You know what I believe, Tessa? That the whole affair has been deliberately trumped up by Connie to serve her own ends. Oh, I'm not denying that Belinda was in the shop, or that she'd broken a few rules, but that's no novelty. They all do it and there's nothing particularly dishonest about it."

"But isn't the place kept locked up out of business hours?"

"Yes, and Patsy has charge of the key, so you can guess how strictly that's guarded. Quite apart from leaving it around in full view, they can usually talk her into letting them borrow it for special occasions, like today, when some kind of celebration is called for. Connie must know that as well as anyone, only naturally it wouldn't suit her to admit it. She's seized on this as an excuse to square her own conscience and prove to us all just how right she was to chuck Belinda out."

"You really think as badly of her as that, Teeny?"

"You bet I do. Everyone was really upset about her

firing one of the most promising pupils ever to enter those portals. Not only Madam, but all of us. And of course she can't take criticism in any form, so now we'll all have to bow down and admit she was right. Belinda not only committed the cardinal sin of becoming penniless, she has proved herself to be a thief and a liar as well. That'll be the story."

I considered this for a while and came to the conclusion that, despite never having personally seen Connie in such a sinister light, Tina had indisputably had opportunities to see sides of her character which had been denied to me and that she was most likely right. However, a small doubt still remained and I said:

"I expect what you say is true and I've been getting hints on all sides, ever since I arrived here, that she's rapidly going round the bend, particularly where money is concerned. And I've had a little first-hand evidence of it too. That lunch we had today would have kept the average family in caviare for a year, and yet nobody has really been able to explain why it's happened. After all, it's not so long ago since you and I used to see her practically every day of our lives and it was never any secret that she was a tyrant and a snob, but when it came to practicalities she always had her feet firmly on the ground. She didn't go around behaving as though she'd just won the pools. So how do you account for this extraordinary transformation?"

"How would I know?" Tina replied indifferently. "She's not well, we're all beginning to realise that, so presumably the illness has affected her brain as well."

"But, as you've just implied, that's a comparatively recent development. Yet Patsy assured me that this dotty extravagance is not new at all. It's been building up for some time."

"You can't tell," Tina began. "People get brain tumours and things which. . . ."

She was obliged to break off at this point because the telephone rang and she had to go into the sitting room to answer it.

The conversation lasted for several minutes, although

Tina's part in it consisted of scarcely a dozen words, all of which were clearly audible:

"Hallo . . . Yes . . . Who? . . . Constance has what? . . . How did . . . ? Yes . . . terrible . . . All right . . . Goodbye."

"That was Madam," she said, walking very slowly back into the kitchen and regarding me with a dazed expression. "The most appalling thing has happened. I still can't take it in, I simply can't."

She bent over, resting her elbows on the draining-board and her head between her hands. "It's just too ghastly and incredible."

"Something has happened to Constance?"

"What? Oh, you heard, did you? She's dead."

"Oh, my Lord! No wonder you're knocked out! When? And how?"

"I'm not really sure. Madam wasn't very coherent. In fact, she was pretty nearly hysterical. She kept yapping on about suicide. I couldn't understand it."

"Not just hysterical, off her head, I should say. Much more likely to have been a straightforward heart attack, don't you think?"

Tina straightened up and stared at me with her mouth falling open:

"Why would she have a heart attack, for God's sake?"

"Oh well, you know, she's been having these black-outs and one thing and another. They must have been more serious than anyone realised. Poor old Connie!"

"Poor old Connie?" Tina repeated on a screeching note, followed by a snort of strangled laughter. "My God, Tessa, I do believe you think I'm talking about Mrs. Bland, don't you?"

"Who else?"

"Constance McGrath, that's who else. You know, you've met her. She's the one they call Hattie."

NINE

Gallantly responding to my urgent summons, Robin and Toby drove over from Roakes Common on Sunday morning and arrived in the lounge of the Nag's Head punctually at half past ten, although not in the best of humours at having their day of rest disrupted in this way.

"It can't be helped," I explained. "There is a lot to tell you and I could hardly be expected to go through it twice. Having you both here at one sitting will save us all time. So do listen to this. . . .

"And the ironical part of it is," I concluded, having given a résumé of events, "far from this being the last straw to break the back of Constance Bland, it seems to have done her a world of good. She is rallying magnificently, as she invariably does with a real challenge. The show must go on, sort of thing. And it's got poor Belinda off the hook too. The expulsion order has been lifted, temporarily at any rate. I dare say even the indomitable Constance would have felt there was a little too much rain falling on her parade to have a second scandal on her hands during the festivities."

"You could also say that it bears out the claim that she is going steadily off her head," Toby remarked. "Surely the sane thing would have been to reject the challenge and cancel the parade?"

"I gather that was mooted, but, as she was quick to point out, it would have been a practical impossibility. There are about three hundred people converging on Waterside at this moment and they come from far and wide. Hattie's death wasn't discovered until yesterday evening, much too late to contact every one of them. It would have ended with about half the parents turning up and the other half staying away, which would have been worse than anything."

"Who did the discovering, by the way?"

"It was one of the girls in her house who raised the alarm; Lottie someone or other. They all eat in a communal dining room, but each house has its own table, so if anyone is missing it's quite easy to spot her and Hattie didn't turn up for supper yesterday evening. If it had been any other sort of gathering no one would have blinked an eye, because she seems to have been a law unto herself where timetables were concerned, but this was different. In all the years she'd been at Waterside she'd never been known to miss a meal."

"And where was she found?"

"Over at the art exhibition, eventually. It took rather a long time because naturally Lottie looked in all the obvious, nearly places first, like dormitories and so on. It wasn't until she went back to the dining room to report that a proper search was started, which may have been a pity, although maybe the delay didn't make any real difference. At any rate, Dr. Bland didn't seem to think so, and I suppose he'd be the one to know."

"Was she already dead?"

"No, in a heavy coma. She died on the way to the hospital."

Robin said: "You still haven't told us who actually found her?"

"It was Madam. She said afterwards that she'd had a hunch that's where Hattie would be, but I don't think it was a particularly inspired one. Anyone could see that, next to her appetite, Hattie loved her art. It may even have been the other way round. However, it isn't yet clear whether she stayed there right through the afternoon, or left and went back again. Personally, I incline to the former."

"Why?"

"Because, as I've just implied, I think she was immensely proud of her work; not vain exactly, but proud and sensitive about it. I think she'd have stuck around, so long as there was a chance of any spectators turning up.

Which reminds me: I must try and get to see Patsy tomorrow. There's something I want her to do for me."

"Now, listen, Tessa, you're not by any remote chance contemplating . . . ?"

"Getting mixed up in the affair? Producing the irrefutable evidence that it wasn't suicide? No, certainly not. It's simply that a few hours before her death Hattie had promised to give me one of her drawings. I think she really wanted me to have it too, only it might be a bit tricky explaining that to Constance Bland. Perhaps I should ask Pauline. If I tell her that it's a little secret, just between the two of us, she's bound to co-operate."

"What sort of drawing?"

"It was more of a caricature really; of myself and two others. Very clever and rather cruel."

"Do you believe she committed suicide?" Toby asked.

"Now, Toby, don't encourage her, I beg you!"

"Naturally, I do," I said firmly. "I mean, isn't it obvious? She really had nothing whatever to live for. Except, of course, that she was as jolly as a sandboy, with plenty of money and allowed to do exactly as she pleased, by all accounts. And apart, also, one should add, from the fact that she had enormous talent and the licence to pursue it to her heart's content; not to mention looking forward to art school next term and a future of glory and renown. Well, what I'm trying to say is, if all that doesn't add up to a motive for suicide, I'd like you to tell me what does."

"That's all very fine," Robin said, "but it's only part of the picture, as you've seen fit to present it. There could be another side to this coin."

"Okay, Robin, go ahead and describe it."

"To start with, you say her mother is dead and her father lives so far away that she rarely sees him. Which means that, besides being something of a misfit, she's also virtually an orphan. That might have a particularly depressing effect on an occasion of this sort, when all the other girls have their families swarming down for the celebrations. No doubt, she's had experience of it before and knows so well how they will all break up into merry little self-sufficient groups and she'll be on the outside, a plain, fat loner, with no one of her own. Shall I go on?"

"Please don't!" Toby implored him. "You are breaking my heart."

"Not mine, though," I assured him. "I don't believe Hattie had a vestige of self-pity and I also get the impression that solitude was something she actively sought. You'll have to do better than that."

"All right, try this for size. She is fat and unattractive, and unlikely to grow out of either condition, being a compulsive eater. She may have made light of it to you, but that doesn't convince me that for one of her age it wouldn't have been a worry. Worse than anorexia, in a way, because at least most of them take a sort of mad pride in being so thin and wouldn't swap it for the world. No compensation of that sort for Hattie. In fact, you told us that she'd admitted as much to Vera."

"She had beautiful manners," I said. "I noticed that at once. It was probably being brought up in diplomatic circles which did it, but she was clever about hitting the tactful and flattering note. She paid me a very graceful compliment within a minute of meeting me and when she heard that Vera's migraine had caused her to miss the lunch party it was probably instinctive to pull out some nervous complaint of her own and build up Vera's morale by asking for advice. I don't suppose. . . ."

I tailed off at this point because the door had opened and in came Vera and Eddie, both in a white heat of excitement:

"Now then!" Eddie said, turning to me as soon as the introductions were over. "You who would have been in the upper echelons of the élite of Delphi, does rumour have it right? Is it true that a Waterside girl has jumped in the river and drowned herself, thus putting paid to the jamboree?"

Having corrected him on both points, I gave a brief outline of the true story. Hattie's name meant nothing to him since, being neither pretty nor flirtatious, she had remained far outside his orbit, but Vera collapsed with a shriek on learning the victim's identity.

"I say, hang on, old girl!" Eddie implored her, as she threw herself back on the sofa and then closed her eyes, as though in pain. "No need for hysterics. Ghastly shock and all that, but it's not as though we knew the poor girl."

White to the gills and scarcely moving her lips, Vera whispered:

"Oh yes, we did."

"Oh, really? Did we?"

"Oh yes," Vera repeated, opening her eyes again. "As Tessa has said, she came and spoke to us on the terrace during the interval yesterday, and also she was looking after the art show when I went in there. It is all so clear to me now. Oh, why did I not say a word about this before? If only I had spoken, perhaps it could have been prevented. Now I must carry some of the blame."

"Why's that? Did she tell you she was planning to kill herself as soon as you left?" Toby asked in tones of mildest curiosity. I could tell that he was already bored by these histrionics and was hoping to cool them, but he had reckoned without Vera, who elected to take the question seriously:

"Oh no," she said, leaning forward and opening her magnificent eyes as wide as they would go. "Do you imagine I am such a wicked fool that I would have kept silent about such a thing? No, she did not tell me, and yet in some way I feel I should have guessed. There was some shadow there. It was my wretched intuition . . . instinct, call it what you like."

"Toby's expression indicated that his name for it would not have been either of these, but Eddie said with immense relief:

"Oh well, that's all right then. Now listen, you lot, why not repair to the privacy of our room, where tooth mugs abound, and push the boat out an inch or two? Too early to order a drink down here on the Sabbath, however much Tessa may bat her eyes at the landlord, but I always keep a flask concealed in my handkerchief drawer."

"What exactly did your instinct or intuition tell you?"

Robin asked, ignoring Eddie's attempt to head Vera off, which I thought was rather unkind of him.

"It is so hard to put into the right words. My English is not always good."

"There you are, then!" Eddie chipped in at once. "Better not try, that's my advice. Slippery customers, these instincts and intuitions. Always creeping up on you uninvited and then leaving you in the lurch when you need them."

However, Robin and Vera now seemed to have entered into a private world of their own, for they both ignored him and continued to speak exclusively to each other. Perhaps he was hoping that she would come up with some new and genuine motive for suicide, thereby scotching any ideas I might have about alternatives, for he said:

"But you definitely did get the impression that all was not well? Why was that? Did she tell you she was depressed? Unhappy?"

"No, it was not so definite. Just a feeling I had."

"What feeling?"

"That here is someone very lonely, with everything bottled up inside and no one to confide in. She was so plain and untidy-looking too, which must have been hard for her at Waterside, where looks count for so much."

"Then I really believe you have nothing to worry about," Robin said, all at once appearing to lose interest. "And you certainly shouldn't blame yourself in any way. How could you possibly have foreseen that she would kill herself, still less have taken steps to prevent it, when all you had to go on were such vague impressions?"

I had seen him use these tactics before, though never with such a casebook response as Vera's:

"This is not all I had," she replied sharply. "There was reason too for what you call these vague impressions."

"Oh yes?"

"You would like to hear?"

"As you wish."

"Or, better still, why not thrash it out over a snort upstairs?" Eddie suggested. "More comfortable, what?"

"If she had not been so lonely as I am telling you," Vera continued relentlessly, "why would she have talked to me as she did? Why does she have to confide in someone who is an absolute stranger?"

"In what way did she confide in you?"

"By telling me how much she hates being so fat and how, in spite of this, she is still unable to stop herself from eating. She is almost in tears about it and asking my advice, which I try my hardest to give her. But what I should have done, if it has not been for this terrible headache, was to realise how serious it was and how near she has become to being desperate."

"Yes, I see," Robin said thoughtfully. "That does put rather a different complexion on it. So you honestly believe she was in a really bad state?"

I wondered that he should encourage her in these fatuous excesses, since it must have struck anyone who had spent two minutes in Vera's company that her chief driving force was self-dramatisation. Having talked to Hattie myself immediately after Vera left, I knew the version we had just heard to be the wildest flight of fancy and I was convinced that, as with her migraine, it was just another device for focusing attention on herself.

Eddie's reactions, on the other hand, were more surprising. For the second time in two days, to my personal knowledge, his tiresome wife had succeeded in knocking him off balance and he was literally twitching with embarrassment at the performance she was throwing together now. He made at least three more attempts to put an end to it by getting us all upstairs for a drink, but it was not until he received some active support from Toby that the breakthrough was achieved.

Robin and I were the last to leave the room and I paused in the doorway to allow the others to go ahead, before muttering:

"And if you believe you now have proof that Hattie killed herself, you must be daft, Robin. I should call Vera about the most unreliable witness who ever crossed your path."

"Oh, I wasn't trying to prove anything," he replied meekly. "I was simply curious to see how far she would have to go before Eddie literally throttled her into silence."

TEN

(1)

As I had foreseen, Robin and Toby flatly refused to sit through either of the two winning performances, although they did undertake to put in an appearance at the prize-giving ceremony after tea. Weather permitting, this was to be held in the garden, with the circular veranda serving as a platform. Needless to say, with Constance Bland in command, the weather that day was sublime.

The brunt of the prize-giving had been allotted to Eddie, with one of the governors backing up with special awards for essays and things of that sort, but one small task had been reserved for me, namely to present the cup for the best drama entry.

A local farmer had been bludgeoned into lending his meadow, on the opposite side of the road to the main Waterside entrance, but parking space was still at a premium, so I accepted Eddie's offer of a lift with him and Vera. Inevitably, during the journey the subject of Hattie's death cropped up again and Eddie said he supposed there would have to be an inquest. When I assented he started plying me with questions as to when it was likely to be and whether we should be required to attend. These were matters on which he would have done better to consult Robin, but since he had omitted to do so, I promised to try and let him have the answers before he left for London.

To my relief, Vera had become very subdued now and hardly contributed a word to this discussion, although she could not resist casting sighs and mournful looks at the sign outside the art exhibition, as we passed it on our way to the theatre. I noticed that it was still open for business, indicating that Connie had not lost her nerve and that it would take more than the sudden death of the principal exhibitor to upset her schedule.

Seats had been reserved for us in the front row, but I remained in mine only long enough to shuffle through the programme and ascertain that it contained no mention of an understudy taking over from Belinda Jameson. Then, explaining to the Harpers that I intended to put this performance to the acid test by viewing it from the back of the circle, I got up and made my way through the foyer and out into the sunlight again.

The cucumber sandwiches girl was on duty this time, but luckily she was showing some other visitors round and they were all standing with their backs to the entrance, surveying the portrait of Hattie's father.

Dipping the desk pen into the silver inkstand, to lend a touch of verisimilitude to the proceedings, I turned back the page of the open Visitors' Book and studied the previous day's entries.

It was by no means a certainty that anyone who had gone there with any but innocent motives would have left a written record of the fact, but, on the other hand, so long as there was a chance of having been seen going inside, attempting to conceal the fact by not signing might have aroused still more suspicion. Moreover, Hattie, with her vested interest at stake, had been extremely diligent on this point and was unlikely to have let anyone off.

There were only three signatures below my own, those of Norah Patterson, Edward Harper and Tina Blundell, in that order. It was a pity that they had not been required to state the exact time of their visits, but at least the position of Eddie's name between the other two made it safe to assume that all three had arrived separately. This could hardly be described as a world-shaking discovery and yet, as I took a last look at the page before turning it over again, I had the nagging feeling that there was some significance to be found in it, if only I could nail it down. It continued to elude me, however, and just then the cucumber girl's voice came floating out behind me, all clear tones and careful diction:

"She's not here just at present, unfortunately," she was saying. "Poor girl was taken ill yesterday and had to be whipped off to the hospital. But I'll tell her what you said and I know she'll be awfully thrilled."

There was no saying whether the speaker believed her own words or not, because even Waterside acting standards were high enough for a statement of that kind, however untruthful, to come tripping of the tongue without a stammer or blush; but, in any case, it sounded as though Connie's delaying tactics were succeeding and that if, by any chance, the press had been tipped off, the news must have come in too late to catch the Sunday papers.

On my way out I came face to face with Madam coming in. She appeared to be in a great hurry, but pulled up when she saw me, looking startled and annoyed.

"What's the matter?" she demanded. "What's wrong now?"

"Nothing much," I replied. "As far as I know."

Her expression changed to one of nervous confusion.

"I do beg your pardon, Miss Crichton . . . you must think me . . . this is the second time . . . the fact is, I thought you were over at the theatre."

"Strictly speaking, I should be, but my presence isn't really necessary this afternoon and I wanted to take a last look at Hattie's pictures."

She accepted the challenge, saying: "So you've heard?"

"Yes."

"May I ask who from?"

"Tina told me."

"Ah yes, she would have, of course."

"I'm staying with her, as you know, so it would have been rather difficult for her to have kept it from me."

"Oh yes, I quite see that; and in any case I don't really approve of all this hushing up."

"Why not?"

"Because it simply isn't practical. You can't keep a thing of that kind hidden for long. There'll be countless rumours flying round before the day is out and in the end that will do even worse damage."

"You're probably right," I admitted. "Someone in the hotel at Gillsford has already got hold of a story about a girl here having drowned herself."

"Pity she didn't, if you ask me," Madam said crisply. "I've no wish to be callous, but it would have made it slightly easier to pass it off as an accident. As it is . . ."

"You don't think it can have been?"

While we talked she had been moving backwards, a step or two at a time and appearing to do so almost unconsciously, but I guessed that it was a deliberate precaution against our being overheard and she did not answer my question, except by a slight shake of the head.

"And I suppose no one yet knows how it happened?" I asked, keeping pace with her gradual retreat.

"Not that I've heard. The . . . examination was to be carried out this morning. They invited Dr. Bland to attend, but I don't think he's back yet. And now, if you'll excuse me, I must leave you. I've got rather a lot on my plate today and I'm running late, as it is."

She turned her back on me and walked away, not very rapidly, but with her effortless, yet purposeful, catlike movement showing to great advantage, and I reflected that whatever had brought her in such a hurry to the art exhibition had not, after all, been so very pressing.

(2)

Three hours later the final curtain came down on the Waterside festivities and there must have been a welcome slowing down of pulses for all those in the know when, with gathering momentum, the parents and visitors drifted away down the drive and still no whisper having circulated concerning Hattie's death.

Mrs. Bland had borne up amazingly well and, so far as I could tell, there had not been a single spasm or fainting fit to mar the regal image. Game to the end, she stood by the front door, shaking hands and bestowing smiles on the favoured, carefully averting her eyes from those not quite grand enough to merit this mark of attention.

Her husband was no less heroic. He remained at her side, exchanging good-humoured remarks with everyone who passed, the very picture of a friendly, benign man who had just spent the jolliest afternoon imaginable and acting the part so skilfully that he almost convinced me that, after all, Hattie had died from natural causes.

The Harpers had been among the first to leave and Robin and Toby, as I discovered too late, had also slunk away in a rather deceitful fashion immediately after the prize-giving ceremony. Doubtless, each party had assumed I would be going with the other, but in fact I found myself faced with the prospect of a four-mile tramp to Gillsford, or else tracking Tina down and hanging about until she was ready to leave.

Being already hot and tired, it was not a difficult choice and I was in luck too, because she had left her car in the same place as before and it was unlocked. After a wait of only ten minutes, just long enough for the bulk of the traffic in the meadow to be on its way and out of ours, she climbed into the driving seat, with the familiar grim expression clouding her face.

"That was quick," I told her. "I had resigned myself to languishing here for at least half an hour."

"It would have been all of that, if Robin hadn't telephoned."

"Telephoned you?"

"No, it was Pauline who took it. The Harpers had just got back to the hotel and he realised there'd been some mix-up over your transport. He wanted you to stay put until he could get over to fetch you."

"Did you speak to him?"

"No, Pauline told him to leave everything to her and she'd drive you there herself; and then of course got into a screaming panic when she couldn't find you. So I thought it was time I took over."

"That was very decent of you. How did you guess where I'd be?"

"It was very simple really. I enquired around and Madam told me she'd seen you getting into my car. Perhaps she's keeping tabs on you."

"Why would she do that?"

"No idea, but I was watching her while you handed out that massive great silver goblet and she was looking at you in a rather peculiar way. I get the impression of a little hostility there."

"It's mutual. Anyway, thanks for coming to the rescue."

She did not reply, probably because we had now caught up with the line of parental cars heading in the direction of Gillsford and the driver in front of us belonged to that erratic variety who need careful watching. About a mile further on, when we had passed the junction with the main road to London and conditions were back to normal, she said:

"It seems she was taking slimming pills."

"Hattie was? How do you know?"

"Patsy found them when she was packing up her belongings. They were wrapped in an oily rag inside the precious box where she kept her paints and brushes. The bottle was almost full, but all the same it does suggest that she was a lot more worried about her weight than she let on."

"Were they quite harmless?"

"No one knows yet. The police have taken them away for analysis."

"You mean to say the police have been there, crawling all over the place and still no one realised there was anything amiss? It's incredible!"

"No, it's not, since they evidently escaped even your vigilant eye. Besides, they weren't crawling all over the place. There were just two men in plain clothes, being very circumspect, at the express request of one of our most prominent and distinguished ratepayers. Furthermore, Connie had already laid on about half the local police force to do car park duty, so one more Panda lurking in the drive wouldn't have raised any comment. She really has all the luck, that woman."

"Well, let's hope it holds up for her until after the inquest, because that's when she'll really be needing some. Posh school, Ambassador's daughter; even Connie won't be able to stop the media making a picnic of that. It'll be bad enough if the verdict is suicide, but . . ."

"What else could it be?"

"Who knows? Murder, perhaps."

'Oh, honestly, Tessa! You shouldn't let your lurid imagination get out of hand, you know. Who in the world would have wanted to murder Hattie?"

"I could name several people."

"Are you being serious?" she asked, turning her head to glare at me with eyes which practically touched. It did not make for a very safe passage over Gillsford Bridge, now thronged with loitering Sunday visitors, and I watered the statement down a little.

"Improbable as it may sound, Teeny, there is nearly always someone who stands to gain by another person's death. In my case, I suppose it would most likely be my understudy, unless there is some passionate policewoman secretly in love with Robin. I don't know who yours would be."

"There wouldn't be anyone, so speak for yourself. If I were to drop off the hook tomorrow, I hope there'd be one or two tears shed, but I can't think of a single individual who'd be glad. I'm not nearly important enough for that and neither was Hattie. Apart from Connie Bland, who's probably cracked anyway, the only one who took her seriously was Pauline and you can be quite sure that was only because she's too frightened of her mother to take an opposite view on any subject."

Her last words coincided with our arrival outside the Nag's Head and she pulled on the handbrake with a mighty tug, as though to emphasise that the subject was now closed. However, since I was no longer taking my life in my hands by contradicting her, I decided to re-open it an inch or two:

"That may be true," I said, "but the fact remains that it is rapidly becoming clear to me that Hattie was very important indeed. Probably the most potentially powerful and dangerous female in the whole of Waterside."

ELEVEN

(1)

Toby was reclining in a deck-chair in a corner of the hotel's rather scruffy little back garden, with his head in a newspaper.

"Back so soon?" he enquired, dropping it on to the grass.

"No thanks to you!"

"Yes, an unfortunate misunderstanding. What are your plans now? Are you staying on in this hotbed?"

"No, I shall go back to London. My work here is done."

"Really? From those rather heavy hints you let fall this morning, one had the impression that it had only just begun. There's a policeman on your track, by the way."

"Do you refer to Robin?"

"No, this one is called Dexter. Robin is out; watching the boats going through the lock. He likes to study human nature in all its many guises."

"I know. What did this Dexter want?"

"Just checking up, I gather. That's to say, on all the people who were in contact with the wretched girl just before her demise."

"Did he tell you that?"

"No, I had it from Eddie, who had just been dragged through the mill himself. Not best pleased about it either, having been collared as he was setting off for London."

"Was Vera checked on too?"

"No, and that was why he was in such a stew. It appears that Vera has been overcome by yet another migraine and they were in a hurry to get home. Eddie had to answer for her, which is something I should not care to do myself. But at least it shows how unjust you were to accuse her of feigning these attacks to get into the act. All it did this time was to keep her out of it."

"What do you think of her, really?"

"Nothing whatever. I have better things to think about."

"Personally, I find something altogether phoney about her."

"If I hadn't better things to think about, I'd probably agree with you."

"I even have moments of doubting whether she's a genuine, *bona fide* Iron Curtain refugee and, whatever you say, I'm certain the migraine is partly put on. I was talking to Billy Bland about it, in a general way, at lunch yesterday and he told me that migraine is not an affliction that people slip in and out of as easily as trying on clothes. You get a lot of warning, as a rule, before an attack, and once you've got it you're stuck with it for anything up to thirty-six hours. Still, I agree that I may have been doing Vera an injustice by saying that she only uses it to draw attention to herself. To be fair, it's probably equally useful for getting her out of things she doesn't want to do."

A waiter appeared on the terrace and then came across the grass towards us.

"Your turn now," Toby said. "This, presumably, is the Dexter summons."

It was a summons of a kind, but not the one we had been expecting. It appeared that I was wanted on the telephone. He did not know the caller's name, but, since there was only one person besides Toby who was up to date on my whereabouts, it came as no surprise to hear Tina's voice on the line.

"They've got the results of the post-mortem," she announced in a tight and rasping voice. "Thought you might be interested."

"Oh, I am. What was it?"

"Sodium nitrate."

"What's that?"

"Highly dangerous chemical, apparently, even in small doses."

"How very strange!"

"But not unheard of, they tell me. There was a case in Oxford a couple of years ago. Some student, I gather. Still, he was known to be on drugs, so it's not quite the same."

"What form does it come in?"

"Tablets for one. Could be mistaken for something harmless, like aspirin."

"Or slimming pills?"

"Yes, but that would mean . . . Oh well, no use speculating at this stage. I just rang to pass on the news, knowing you'd be gasping for it."

"How did you hear?"

"Madam told me. The telephone was ringing when I walked into the flat."

"How's she taking it?"

"Not very cheerfully, as you might expect. Listen, Tessa, it's been great fun seeing you again and let's keep in touch and all that, but I've got to hang up now. Connie Bland has called a staff meeting for eight o'clock and God knows when I'll be back, but when you come to collect your stuff, do remember not to walk off with the keys."

I had been thinking fast during this conversation and now asked her:

"Are you throwing me out, by any chance?"

"No, of course not. What on earth are you on about?"

"That's what it sounded like."

"Well, it wasn't intentional. It simply never occurred to me that you wouldn't be going back to London this evening. Do you mean you want to stay on?"

"If it's not inconvenient?"

There was silence for a moment or two and then she said coolly:

"Not in the least; I'm deeply flattered. Okay, in that case, I'll see you later. Bye for now."

It was not the most ecstatic of welcomes and I concluded that her feet, as Miss Lawrie would have put it, had warned her that she was making a mistake, but on this occasion had been over-ruled by her Waterside training in manners.

There was a tall, dejected-looking man lurking in the lobby when I emerged from the telephone kiosk and he came up to me, enquired my name and introduced himself as Sergeant Dexter, all of which was superfluous because I would have recognised that particular lurk from a mile off.

"Sorry to bother you like this, but if you could just spare me a few minutes? I thought we might sit in here," he said, producing a key and unlocking the door of the Lounge Bar, this being five-thirty p.m. He then ushered me inside and relocked the door behind us. He had a diffident manner, a low, soft voice and a friendly, rather appealing smile, but conceivably all these traits had been cultivated purposely to disarm people and encourage indiscretions, so I cautioned myself to keep my guard up, while at the same time adopting an eager, co-operative expression when, having glanced through some notes, he said:

"I am here in connection with the death of Constance McGrath of Waterside School. Just a few preliminaries to get out of the way first, if you'd be so good. Is Theresa Crichton your full name?"

"My professional name," I explained. "I'm an actress, you see. I don't normally sign myself in that way, but it happens to be the name I'm known by at Waterside. I was at school there, for one thing."

"Yes, I gathered. And your non-professional name?"

"Theresa Price," I replied and left it at that, having decided it would be safer to omit any reference to Robin. If by some remote chance, the Sergeant's confidence was really so shaky as appearances suggested, it might have collapsed altogether on learning that he was interrogating the wife of a Scotland Yard Inspector, and it could have ended with his hustling me out of the room in a courteous fashion before I had learnt anything at all.

"And your address?"

"At present it is Flat 3, Queen Anne House, Gillsford."

"Really? You live in Gillsford?"

"No, I live in London, but I'm staying here for a few days. My permanent address is 51, Beacon Square, S.W.1."

"It seems to me that I've come across that Gillsford address somewhere before," he said when he had written all this information down. "Ah yes, here we are! Tina Blundell, Assistant Ballet Mistress. Would that be right?"

"Quite right. She didn't mention that I was staying with her?"

"I haven't had a chance to speak to her yet," he replied sadly, as though the omission was a matter for lamentation. "Getting the addresses of the non-resident staff was simply routine, but at the moment we're concentrating on people outside the school who were known to have been in contact with Constance within a short time of her death. I see from the Visitors' Book that you were one of them."

"That's true, although not by any means the last. I went round the exhibition immediately after lunch."

"Nevertheless, whatever you are able to tell us may be of some help. I understand you had a rather special relationship with her?"

"Who told you that?" I asked, a fraction more sharply than I had intended.

"We found this," he replied, handing me a stiff brown envelope, "tucked inside the Visitors' Book. There's no name on the envelope, as you see, but we think it must have been intended for you."

I opened it and drew out the sketch which Hattie had captioned "Judgement Day". Something had been added since I last saw it and the blank space below the three heads was now covered with the following message, in large, flamboyant script:

"To T.C., with admiration, love and gratitude, C.M."

Being sentimental by nature, it was no surprise to find the tears starting to my eyes.

"I told her I would hang it in my dressing room," I explained, blinking them away. "And I will too."

"Not just yet, though, if you don't mind awfully," the Sergeant said, holding out his hand. "We'd rather like to hang on to it for a few hours, if you've no objection?"

For all his winning ways, it was hard to believe that any objection I could have raised would have made a jot of difference, so I handed the drawing back without a word and he went on:

"Do you deduce anything from the fact that we found it where we did? Also that it had been neatly parcelled up, as it were?"

I thought it over for a minute and then said:

"Presumably, you are suggesting that she was anxious that it should get to me, but knew she wouldn't be around to see to it herself, since she intended to commit suicide. Is that what you're saying?"

"No, I'm not saying it, I'm asking you."

"Then the answer is No. I don't think anything of the kind."

"You sound very positive," he said sorrowfully, as though acknowledging with some regret that this was not an epithet which could be applied to himself.

"I am because, although I wouldn't describe it as a special relationship, I did talk to Hat . . . Constance on two occasions before that last one and each time she struck me very forcibly as someone who enjoyed life immensely and was looking forward with confidence to the future. As for putting her sketch inside an envelope and then into the book, if you'd ever met her you'd realise that it had quite another significance. The fact is, she took her work very seriously and would have taken great trouble to protect it."

"Yes, I see. Well, I'm most grateful and I'll certainly bear your remarks in mind. You'll probably be pleased to hear that they almost mirror the impressions of Mr. and Mrs. Harper."

My astonishment on hearing this was so profound that it must have been revealed in my expression and I hastily attempted to account for it by asking:

"Oh, have you talked to them as well? I thought they'd gone back to London?"

"They have now, I believe. It seems Mrs. Harper wasn't at all well. Suffers from migraine, poor lady, but Mr. Harper was kind enough to spare me a few minutes and he was able to speak for his wife as well. Neither of them had exchanged more than a few words with Constance and they hadn't noticed anything at all out of the ordinary in her behaviour."

"Which suggests that it must have been an accident?"

"One certainly wouldn't care to think of such a young person being driven to take her own life," he replied smoothly, evidently taking no account of a third alternative, and I did not mention it either. For one thing, I was not even sure that it would have been grammatical.

"By the way," he said in a voice of deep sadness, while unlocking the bar door, "I think you must be the Theresa Crichton who's married to Robin Price?"

"Yes, I am. Don't tell me you know him."

"Know him? Oh yes, I think you could say that. Known him . . . must be getting on for twenty years now."

(2)

"A thumping exaggeration, I need hardly tell you," Robin said, "but typical of Dexter. He enjoys dropping his tiny bombshells and is not above using a dash of poetic licence to enhance the effect."

"You do surprise me! I had him down as a very sobersided, unimaginative sort of man. How long have you actually known him?"

"Eight or nine years would be nearer the mark. Just before you bobbed up in my life, in fact. We used to meet fairly regularly when I was at Storhampton. There were numerous occasions when our territories overlapped."

"He must be pretty dim if he's still a sergeant eight or nine years later?"

"Or rates euphony above promotion?" Toby suggested. "Inspector Dexter, after all? It has an element of the absurd."

"Not dim at all," Robin said. "It's just that something in his temperment or nervous system got switched off a few years ago. Domestic troubles."

"What happened?"

"His wife ran off with someone else. Said she couldn't stand the unsocial hours. Silly fool! Why marry a police-man if what you really want is someone who comes home at five o'clock every evening and gets ready to take you to the golf club dinner?"

"Why, indeed?" I agreed. "How did the social hours suit her?"

"Badly. The other man left her after a couple of years and she slipped quietly out with an overdose. Tiresome woman! Needless to say, Dexter blames himself for the whole silly shambles."

We had adjourned to Tina's flat by this time and were awaiting her return, hoping for more first-hand news from Waterside. The plan was for Toby to drop Robin off at the main line station, so leaving the car for me, although I had promised that both of us would be back in London before the end of the week. In the meantime, he was sitting out the delay quite amiably and I half suspectd him of being almost as eager as I was to hear Tina's report on the emergency staff meeting.

"Why do you suppose Eddie misquoted Vera so outrageously?" I asked, hoping to fan this flame, if it did exist, into a bigger blaze. "You both heard her going on about what a state poor Hattie was in and how it came as no surprise that she had decided to end it all. Yet Eddie flatly contradicted that when he was reporting to the Sergeant and insisted that neither of them had noticed the slightest thing wrong."

"Either because he guessed there was no truth in the version she gave us," Robin answered, "and that she was simply showing off, or else . . ."

"What?"

"Or else he was afraid she would repeat the act, to impress Dexter, who might take it seriously and feel it necessary to call her as a witness at the inquest. Eddie would have wished to avoid that at all costs and I dare say Vera was also beginning to get cold feet by then and had settled for another migraine and for letting Eddie do the talking."

"Yes, I should say that's the most likely explanation. I have a feeling there is nothing very spontaneous about these outbursts of Vera's. I believe that nearly everything she does is calculated, but the trouble is that it's usually done so clumsily that she has to get Eddie to rush in and smooth things over for her."

"I'm not quite with you," Robin said.

"And, if I were you, I'd stay right where you are," Toby advised him. "I scent trouble when she heads off into these marital relationship jungles."

"To give you just one example," I persisted. "When Vera learnt that Hattie was dead, her immediate reaction was to try and convince everyone that it was suicide. It was only later on, when the damage had been done, that she realised how much more discreet it would have been to sit tight and say nothing. In that way, no one would ever have felt the need to seek a connection."

"A connection between what, for God's sake?"

"Why, Hattie and Vera, of course. What else have we been talking about?"

"On rather different levels though, if you'll forgive my saying so. This is the first I've heard of any connection between them."

"I gave you my advice," Toby reminded him, "and you would have done well to listen to it. When it pleases Tessa to have a connection she will find one, and if it does not exist she will invent it."

"I am not inventing anything this time," I told him. "The signs are all there for those with eyes to see."

"Then I must be blind," Robin said, "for I was under the impression that Vera had never set foot in Waterside before and had scarcely clapped eyes on Hattie until they had their little chat at the exhibition, which you are the first to admit was largely a fiction, anyway."

"I admit all that," I agreed, adding, after a suitable pause for effect. "But on the other hand, I am pretty sure that Hattie knew Vera or, rather, knew a great deal more about her than Vera could have dreamed of, far less desired, and that Vera discovered this yesterday afternoon."

"And what is the basis for this melodramatic theory?"

"Visual evidence, as it happens. It still exists, but unfortunately I can't show it to you just at present, so you'll have to take my word for it. You see, when Sergeant Dexter handed me Hattie's caricature just now, he only gave enough time to identify it, before snatching it back again, but you know how it is with pictures? If they have any merit at all, something invariably strikes you at a second viewing which you missed the first time and that's how it was with this one. I looked only at the head at the top of the drawing, which was Vera's of course, and straightaway I noticed something distinctly odd and suggestive about it."

At this point, I paused once again, to give proper gravity and emphasis to my next words and immediately had cause to regret it. In the small silence, while Robin and Toby regarded me with appropriate degrees of curiosity and scepticism, we heard a key turning in the lock, followed by a voice calling:

"Anyone at home? If so, you can put a hot-water bottle in my bed and fetch the Valium."

TWELVE

(1)

"You never saw such a carry-on in your life," Tina told us, when she had been revived by a stiff dose from the whisky bottle which Robin had thoughtfully brought along. "It was supposed to be a staff meeting, to put us in the picture about Hattie, but it developed into a ruddy brawl. They did everything except throw the furniture about."

"Do tell us!" I begged her.

"Well, it was all set off by a stupid little misunderstanding. Madam mentioned something about Constance, meaning Hattie, of course; but you know how she persists in waging this private war against the Waterside nicknames? Anyway, Connie Bland, who was already in a state of controlled dither about this blot on the escutcheon, chose to take it as a reference to herself and she fairly let fly. Told Madam she could mind her own business and remember who she was talking to and various other cutting remarks on those lines. It was frightfully embarrassing, but I suppose it proves that we were right, Tessa. Connie has known all along about Billy and Madam, only it suited her to close her eyes to it. All the same, she must have been seething with jealous fury underneath, and bottling it up hasn't improved her temper. So now, when she feels that she and her beloved school are under threat from all sides, one more pinprick is enough to send her berserk."

"So then what happened?" I asked.

"Things went from bad to worse. Instead of explaining her mistake and patching things up, Madam launched into a slanging match on her own account. She accused Connie of being a tryant and a megalomaniac, among other things, and she also got in a dig about her extravagance and how we were all obliged to sit meekly by and wait for the crash. Perfectly true, of course, but hardly the moment to bring that up."

"And hardly relevant to the subject you were supposed to be discussing?" Robin suggested.

"Quite. She did allude to Hattie at one point, although unfortunately she managed to imply that that was Connie's fault too. If she hadn't spoilt her rotten and so on and so forth, this disaster could have been averted. She never had any time for Hattie herself, so she was getting in a double blow there. I simply can't imagine what got into her. Of course, I realise that she's been under enormous strain too, but it really was unforgivable and she even tried to rope poor old Patsy in to back her up, which was a bit mean. Whatever Patsy may mutter in private, it would be more than her life was worth to criticise Connie openly."

"How did she get out of it?"

"Rather cleverly really, although it probably wasn't calculated. She started to cry, which is exactly what most of the girls do when they've been caught out and tears are the only defence left. Still, I dare say these were genuine tears. The whole rotten business was enough to make anyone weep."

"So there's the picture," I said, "Connie and Madam hurling insults at each other like a couple of fishwives, Patsy sobbing quietly in her corner, while the rest of you sit around biting your nails. I can't quite place Billy, though. Presumably, he was there, being a partner in the firm, so to speak? He must have found himself in a rather ticklish situation?"

"Probably did, but you know Billy. He usually manages to slide out when things start hotting up and this time his escape route was practically handed to him on a plate with watercress round it. At one point Connie was temporarily overcome by a choking fit. I expect it was pure rage, as a matter of fact, because she soon recovered, but it was slightly alarming while it lasted and Billy was on his feet in a trice, saying he'd fetch her a glass of water. I need hardly say that he was able to spin out that little task for at least ten minutes. The worst was over by the time he got back and things had simmered down a bit."

"Yes, typical Billy manouevre," I agreed. "But has anything emerged from this meeting? Did the subject of sudden death and sodium nitrate ever get an airing?"

"It was touched on towards the end, but only in a general way. We were told that the inquest was to be on Wednesday and, acting on instructions, Pauline had sent telegrams to all the parents, informing them that owing to unforeseen circumstances, term will end ten days early and all the girls who can't be collected personally will be on the nine-forty to Paddington on Wednesday morning."

"How many telegrams would that have required?" Toby asked her.

"Eighty, at least, and that must have cost a bomb or two."

"It's a wonder your old Madam didn't ask whether a second-class stamp wouldn't do just as well," I remarked, "but I begin to feel sorry for Connie, I really do. Not that she'd care a damn about the expense, but it must have been a terrible blow to her pride to admit that something could go so terribly wrong at wonderful Waterside."

"She hadn't much alternative. Hattie's father is already on his way from South America and, with the inquest and everything, there wouldn't be a hope of hushing it up. Things would have got completely out of hand with all the girls on the premises, gossiping and goggle-eyed and their mothers ringing up every ten minutes to enquire if they were still alive. Now, with an extra-long summer holiday ahead, there'll be time for the sting to go out of it and I doubt if many of them will actually remove their little darlings."

I could only hope she was right, although I had a nasty suspicion that sooner or later we should be in for a much bigger and more damaging scandal than any that had so far occurred to her. I said:

"Yes, I am sure it was the only way out and you can't accuse her of doing things by halves. In fact, you could say that the whole ghastly business has brought out all the old fighting spirit. Even her health seems to have bucked up."

"Oh no, it hasn't," Tina said with one of her mirthless snorts. "You haven't heard the curtain line yet."

"We all waited for her to give it to us, one at least with bated breath.

"You remember that black-out Connie had at your luncheon party, Tessa? Well, from the way you described it, I should say that exactly the same thing happened this evening. She was talking quite normally, we'd moved on to the business of getting all the heavy luggage down to the station in advance, and then all at once her voice went slurry. She tailed off completely and collapsed in a heap on the table."

"Yes, that's exactly how it was before. But how awful, Tina! Did she pull out of it?"

"Couldn't tell you. Billy bundled us all out of the room; all except Patsy, that is, and Madam also seemed inclined to linger, but there was nothing the rest of us could do, so I got in the car and drove home; and that's the latest news I have."

This reference to getting into cars and driving to places reminded two of the party that there was a train to be caught and I went downstairs to see them off. On the way Robin said in a voice brimming with insincerity:

"Bad luck, Tessa! You never got your punch line in, after all, did you? I'm afraid the old school chum rather stole your big scene."

"It can wait," I replied. "And it may have been just as well. One is apt to become carried away with such a good audience and there's still a remote possibility that I'm mistaken. I shall have to get my hands on a dictionary before I can be certain, and in the meantime. . . ."

"And in the meantime, it might be as well not to go plunging in up to your neck before you've got your facts straight."

"Yes, okay, and while I'm not doing that, there's something you can be doing for me."

Perhaps he felt he had rather overdone the bossy, patronising bit, for he said amiably:

"Yes, if I can."

"Two things really, and by pressing the right buttons they will only take you a couple of ticks. The first is to find out whether Vera possesses, or has even possessed, a driving licence."

"And the second?"

"That's easier still. I'd like to know where an Ambassador called McGrath, now in South America, was posted before that."

(2)

"Tell me something, Teeny," I said, on re-entering the flat a moment or two later. "When Billy Boy eventually brought Connie's glass of water, was it really water, or something else?"

"What do you mean by something else?" she demanded, giving me the Cyclops look.

"Oh well, you know, it could have been brandy or something and that's why it took him so long?"

This was not really what I had in mind, but I thought a half-truth would be less likely to arouse her fury than the whole one. I was wrong though because the fierceness of her reaction was out of all proportion to the question which, on the face of it, I had considered to be harmless enough.

"Oh, I see what you're getting at," she replied in a disgusted voice. "And I know who you've been talking to."

"Do you? Who?"

"Patsy; so don't bother to deny it. She's the only one who could have put that idea into your head."

"The idea that Billy might have given his wife something slightly more stimulating than water, when she'd just had a choking fit and was battling through a crisis? What's so terrible about that?"

"Oh, don't go all babyfaced and innocent, it's not your style. You know very well it's not as simple as that and I must say I'm disappointed."

"May we take this one step at a time?" I asked, for I genuinely had no idea what she was talking about. "First of all, what are you disappointed about?"

"Old Patsy blabbing to you."

"About what?"

"Alcohol being at the root of Connie's trouble, of course. I know that's Patsy's private theory, because she once mentioned it to me, but I never dreamt she'd go spreading it around to all and sundry."

"Well, we seem to be getting somewhere at last," I admitted. "Although I'm not sure I care for the direction we're going in. For one thing, I don't much like being bracketed with all and sundry and, for another, Patsy has never dropped so much as a hint of that kind. I trust I can make you believe that?"

"You'll have to work pretty hard at it."

"Oh, I don't foresee much difficulty," I assured her. "Just listen to this: supposing, for the sake of argument, that Patsy had done the thing you've accused her of and supposing also that I'd thought there was some truth in it, would I then have asked you whether Billy had brought along something stronger than water?"

"Yes, in my opinion, that's exactly what you would have done."

"Are you mad, Teeny? He's a doctor, need I remind you? He'd know better and sooner than anyone if his wife were turning into an alcoholic. How could I imagine he would be so irresponsible as to run around fetching up more of the stuff and literally putting it into her hands?"

"Because, my dear Tessa, knowing you, it would be such a short step from there to assuming that he not only does know, but is actively encouraging her."

A great light dawned and I said:

"Well, I'll be blowed! Damned if I won't!"

"Don't pretend that wasn't at the back of your mind when you played your little opening gambit."

"Cross my heart. It's a totally new concept, so far as I am concerned, but I see now that it's firmly lodged at the back of yours, which is why you jumped on me like a load of bricks. However, that's not why I'm blowed. Do you want the truth?"

"Go ahead, if it amuses you."

"The sordid truth is that my reason for asking what Billy put in the glass was to check whether he had filled it with something which had a strong enough flavour to disguise something else."

After a brief but menacing pause, in which Tina's feet got to work, she said:

"Like sodium nitrate, for instance?"

"Exactly! Isn't that amazing?"

"I don't find it amazing. I call it a much more damaging accusation than the first one."

"Well, of course it is and that's the amazing part. Here

have I been flogging myself into the ground over this complicated theory that Billy is using his expertise to poison his wife by slow degrees and in such a way as to make it look as though she had a heart complaint. So that when she did have a fatal attack, one of his partners would sign on the dotted line and no questions asked. Awfully risky of course, because she could have taken it into her head at any moment to consult a specialist and then Billy really would have been up the spout. Another snag was that poisoning doesn't really match his temperament. There's a long-drawn-out cruelty about it, which is the last thing one associates with him. And now I learn that all the while you've had this perfectly logical, straightforward solution up your sleeve, or inside your dancing shoes, which also explains Connie's reluctance to see another doctor. She would know only too well what was the matter with her and where the cure lay. That's what amazes me. That you should have seen all this and that I could have been so blind."

"I'll thank you to leave me out of your little games, if you don't mind, Tessa. Patsy may have hinted to me that Connie was tipping back the bottle rather too frequently, and I may or may not agree with her. That's entirely my own affair, so kindly don't associate me with this new fantasy you're now building up. Maybe Connie is turning into an alcoholic, but no one has ever suggested that Billy was aiding and abetting her and I think you ought to apologise for such a foul and disgusting insinuation."

Having lectured me in this haughty fashion, she slammed off into the kitchen, where I heard her opening and shutting drawers in a rather frenzied fashion. I got up and prowled around her elegant little sitting room for a few minutes, before joining her. She was peering into a knife drawer and, without looking up, she said:

"Honestly, Tessa, you make me so furious I can't even remember what I came in here to look for. Have you come to apologise?"

"Yes, if you like. I never mind apologising to ostriches. It doesn't carry the same sting."

"Just because I haven't got your beastly, morbid, suspicious mind!"

"It isn't a question of that. It's facts I'm talking about and there's simply no way round them. Either you believe that Connie's illness and personality change are caused by drink, or you don't; and since you evidently do, you have to accept the fact that Billy is encouraging her. The only alternative would be that he simply hasn't noticed, and that I refuse to believe."

"It still doesn't follow that he encourages her."

"Yes, it does, I've seen him at it. There was enough wine on the table last Saturday to float a battleship. Billy was pouring it out himself and he was just as attentive to his wife as to the rest of us. I agree he might find it hard to stop her secreting bottles in the wardrobe, if she had a mind to, but he could certainly keep a tight control over her public drinking. Since he doesn't, one is forced to conclude that the way things are going suits him down to the ground."

"Yes, I suppose I must admit there's a grain of truth in that," Tina said. She was still frowning, but more thoughtfully now than in anger and I could see that she was wavering. "I do recall that on the rare occasions when I've been invited to headquarters to receive a little pat on the back, he's always very lavish with the gin and tonic, and that includes the measures he pours for Connie too; so to that extent I suppose you could call me an ostrich. I lack this facility to put two and two together, far less come up with the right answers. What is the answer, anyway?"

"That he's hoping she'll kill herself, either from straightforward alcoholic poisoning, or by getting so stewed one day that she'll fall down and break her neck."

"I gathered that much, but what you haven't explained is why he should want either of those things to happen. Okay, so he's heavily involved with Madam, but we both know that he's had affairs with lots of women in the past and it has never affected his marriage. Goodness knows, his womanising wasn't a particularly well-kept secret, even from us, but it always seemed that he and Connie had a

perfectly good understanding, so why should all that have
changed now?"

"I can give you several reasons, one being that Madam
is not only exceptionally attractive, but most likely exceptionally ambitious as well. Probably on the look-out for a
husband too, and who better than Billy? There's also the
fact that she's actually living on the premises, which must
give her a lot more scope; but there's something else more
important still. Always in the past giving up Connie would
have meant giving up his share in the school, which, *ipso
facto* as the saying goes, would have meant giving up about
two-thirds of his very substantial income. That doesn't
apply in this case. With her background and experience,
Madam could run the show almost as efficiently as Connie
and I've no doubt that she's itching to get her claws on it.
What's your answer to that?"

Tina did not reply for almost a minute. She had been
peering into the drawer again and now brought out a
wicked-looking paring knife and started tapping the blade
on her thumbnail in a vaguely threatening manner.
However, I did not believe that her venom was any longer
directed at me and, indeed, when she did speak, it was in a
relatively mild tone:

"I have a nasty feeling that for once you could be right,
Tessa. Not that there's much one can do about it, is there?
And I do hope you won't try and fabricate some connection
between this and Hattie's death?"

"As it happens, I was quite serious in saying that I
regarded Hattie as powerful and potentially dangerous. I
have an idea that, from her solitary vantage point, she had
a very sharp view of life; not to mention a strong malicious
streak. However, if it's any consolation to you . . ."

"Yes?"

"If it should turn out to be murder, I'm putting my
money on quite a different horse from Billy or Madam.
Which reminds me: could you do a small job for me? Two,
actually, if we're to eliminate all the other possibilities and
leave dear old Waterside without a stain on its reputation."

"Depends on what you want me to do."

"Just now, while I was trying to find the right words to frame my apology, I looked along your shelves for a dictionary, but you don't seem to have one. Could you borrow the Oxford from the school library?"

"Whatever for?"

"Something I want to look up."

"It's pretty hefty, you know. Wouldn't it be easier if I looked it up for you?"

"No, it wouldn't, and if you're really keen to get your precious old Madam and Billy off the hook, you must stop this incessant quibble."

"Oh, all right. What was the other thing?"

"That may be a little more difficult," I admitted. "Not insuperable, though, and I dare say Patsy would be the one to help us here. There's a sketch of Hattie's which I'd like to borrow for a few hours. It's the one she was working on the very first time I met her: a pen and ink drawing of birds, fish and animals and they all have human faces."

"And what do you expect to glean from that?"

"I honestly don't know yet, Teeny, but I have a feeling that it may contain a vital clue of some kind. There was something curious about her reaction when I came across her that afternoon, on the steps by the river. She was completely poised and sure of herself, in a sense, and yet she gave the impression of having been caught out in something rather wicked. She explained it away by saying that she ought not to be there and would get into trouble if it were found out. It sounded plausible enough at the time, but I've since learnt that she made a practice of wandering off on her own and that, far from its landing her in trouble, Connie herself condoned it and made everyone else do the same."

"Nevertheless, a fairly feeble basis for believing that this drawing had some dark significance."

"That's not all it's based on. There's also the fact that as soon as I turned up she shoved the drawing out of sight, and later on, when I asked to see it, she was genuinely reluctant to let me. Again I was fooled and attributed it to modesty or self-consciousness, but it could hardly have been either of those. Considering her age and appearance, she was remarkably self-possessed and she certainly had no false modesty about her work. In fact, I think it was only because vanity overcame discretion that she finally consented to show it to me."

"Discretion about what?"

"Well, as I've said, Teeny, all these animals had human faces. Some I recognised, others not, but I only had about two minutes to take it in and also that was before I had been indoors and had a chance to meet people again, and revive memories. You'll recall that I didn't even recognise you at first?"

"I still haven't grasped where all this is supposed to be leading us."

"And I'm not perfectly sure myself. I simply have a feeling that this drawing was a device to depict people's personalities and it may have had a bearing on their behaviour as well. Now, if in the case of one person some intimate knowledge as Hattie had shown herself to possess could be extremely damaging . . . well, what I'm driving at is, in that case, can't you see how that person might have reacted on seeing himself or herself portrayed in this way."

"Reacted by murdering her, you mean?"

"Not to put too fine a point on it, yes."

Tina subjected me to one of her terrifying frowns: "In that case, Tessa, isn't all this a complete waste of time?"

"Is it? Why?"

"Because, if Hattie's drawing did contain some damaging evidence of that kind, which personally I find pretty farfetched anyway, but if it did, and if she was killed for that reason, then you can be perfectly certain that the drawing has now been destroyed."

"That's possible, I grant you, but not an absolute certainty. Inspecting the picture would have been one thing, getting one's hands on it quite another. It's extremely unlikely that Hattie would have handed it over on demand. And once she was dead there would have been no end of obstacles. It would have required a very inventive mind to find a plausible excuse for searching through her belongings. Besides, would it really have been necessary? It's quite possible that the sketch would have had no significance at all to anyone who didn't possess that special knowledge. Hattie would have been killed not to get possession of the drawing, but to prevent her passing on that knowledge in a more intelligible form."

"And since, as you say, it's going to require a good deal of ingenuity to search through her belongings, perhaps you'd care to suggest how I should go about it?"

"Yes, that is rather a problem, but I think we can overcome it. Just tell Patsy that Hattie had promised to give me a cartoon she'd done of the three competition judges. No need to add that it's already in the hands of the police."

"And what if she stands over me while I'm looking for it? If I do find the one you want, it won't in the least resemble three judges."

"Oh really, Teeny, haven't you any imagination at all? Surely, after all this time, you know how to con Patsy? Pretend to be bowled over by the drawing and say you'd like to show it to me; or find yourself overtaken by a craving for walnut whips and stick it in your bag while she's rummaging in the cupboard. I'm sure you'll get an inspiration when the time comes."

She continued to grumble for a while, but eventually ran out of objections and reluctantly agreed to do as I asked.

THIRTEEN

Monday morning brought its full quota of ups and downs and there was some of both in Robin's early telephone call.

"Answer to your first question," he said, dispensing with the preamble, "Czechoslovakia."

"Good! That'll do nicely."

"He has also been Minister in Warsaw, First Secretary in Moscow."

"You're a genius, Robin! What about the other thing?"

"Not so positive, I'm afraid. No driving licence."

"Really? None at all? Not even an international one, issued abroad?"

"So far as we can check it, none at all."

"That's a blow. My theory rather hinges on getting from point A to point B."

"With Vera in the driving seat, presumably?"

"That's about it."

"Well, sorry to disappoint you, but I still regard this connection between Vera and Hattie as fragile, to say the least."

"Getting stronger by the minute though. However, I could be wrong. I'm still waiting for confirmation."

"And, having got it, what next?"

"A stroll down to the river perhaps. It's another lovely day."

"Please don't imagine you're fooling anyone," Robin said. "I'd recognise that innocent tone from another planet and it still sends shivers down my spine. What are you up to, really?"

"I would tell you," I assured him, "but I can hear my landlady returning; and bearing gifts, with any luck, so it isn't the moment."

Sure enough, Tina entered the room as I spoke and

when I had transmitted their love back and forth to each other I rang off and turned to her, all eagerness for the news on that front.

In essence, it consisted of one Up and one Down. On the assumption that foul play could not be ruled out, as the saying goes, I had lined up two major candidates for the role of Hattie's murderer and it was my plan to concentrate simultaneously on the motives and opportunity of each, until one should be positively eliminated. In other words, in my eyes, unlike those of the law, both were to be regarded as guilty until one was proved innocent.

The nice balance between them had shifted somewhat during my conversation with Robin, his evidence having reduced Vera's score by several marks, but it soon went soaring up again when Tina handed me the dictionary and I scurried through to the letter S. This provided not only the confirmation I needed, but also consolidated the impression that it had been Hattie's particular amusement to convey her slightly malicious comments in visual terms.

"How about the animal sketch?" I asked, putting the volume on one side. "Have you brought that too?"

Tina shook her head.

"Oh, why not?"

"Because it wasn't there. I did exactly as you suggested, pretending to be looking for a cartoon of three heads, while keeping my eyes peeled for fishes and birds. I must say, I hated myself too. Patsy is so trusting and when she understood it was for your sake she became wildly cooperative and brought out stacks of sketch books and portfolios. I felt such a rat."

"Were there many?"

"Dozens. No, far more than that. Nearer a hundred, I should say. Apparently, Hattie made sketches of all her finished work and she rarely destroyed anything."

"Then how come this one was missing?"

"Presumably, because she hadn't left it at The Lodge."

"Where else could it be?"

"Well, the fact is, Tessa, this isn't as simple as you imagined. For one thing, she was allowed to work in the practise studio, when it wasn't being used for dancing, and she'd left quite a lot of her stuff there. Madam is the queen bee on that territory and she'd asked one of her students to collect it all up and take it over to The Lodge. So, in theory, it was included in the lot I saw, but in practice almost anyone could have removed one or more of the drawings."

"Yes, that's a complication I hadn't bargained for."

"And, as I keep telling you, if Hattie had found out something terribly damaging about someone at Waterside and they had recognised themselves and their crimes in her picture, then obviously they wouldn't have rested until that picture was destroyed. It stands to reason."

I sighed: "Yes, I suppose it does, and you've been proved right, as usual. However, It doesn't wreck my case. It simply widens the field a little and I shall have to take that into account."

"I can't understand why you bother. Why not leave all this kind of thing to the police? It's their job, after all, and they must be far better equipped to deal with it than you are."

"There I can't agree with you. Not wishing to boast, I'll bet you a million pounds that I've acquired more details about Hattie's character and background, not to mention her part in all the Waterside ramifications, than Sergeant Dexter could uncover in a month of blue moons."

"Oh well, if it amuses you, who am I to interfere?" Tina said in her most patronising voice. "Besides, I've got better, or at any rate more urgent, calls on my time."

"Such as?"

"Earning my salary. I've got two classes on my regular schedule and an extra one has been shoved in on top of it."

"You don't seem to get much time off. I thought you told me you only worked there three days a week?"

"In theory, but I'm expected to be a little more flexible when there's a show coming up, and these are exceptional times. We're breaking up ten days early, don't forget, and exams start in the first half of next term, so we've got to pack in as much as possible while we have the chance."

"What a shame! I was hoping we could hire a boat for the afternoon and do a leisurely paddle up the river."

"Sorry, not a hope."

"In that case, I'll just have to try and manage on my own."

"Try not to fall in and drown yourself," Tina said, not sounding too worried about it.

FOURTEEN

Not more than three minutes' walk from the Nag's Head, and situated midway between Gillsford bridge and the lock, there was a boatyard belonging to J. Hobbes & Sons, an old-established family firm, who hired out river craft of every size and variety, for periods ranging from one hour to three weeks.

Even out of season, when business was slack, the chances of finding what I sought would have been thin enough; after a fine weekend in high summer, with customers coming through at the rate of about one party per minute, they were reduced to almost nil. Nevertheless, I still felt it was worth a try and, to some extent at any rate, my luck was in.

This being Monday, the rush had eased off considerably, requiring only the commanding presence of one member of the Hobbes clan to deal with the business end. This was a stout, middle-aged woman with frizzy hair and a kippered complexion. She wore dirty navy blue trousers and a sagging brown cardigan and had a cigarette stuck to her mouth, which she prised off only once during the time I spent with her, and that was in order to light a fresh one. However, after a somewhat brusque reception, she became quite affable, providing me with my first stroke of luck and a fine example of the many blessings which television can bring to contemporary life, for with no help at all she recognised me.

"Don't tell me," she entreated, screwing up her eyes against the smoke. "I know! Got it in one! Theresa Crichton, right?"

After that it was plain sailing, except that she seemed to know a good deal more than I did about the intricacies of television production, for it appeared that Gillsford had become a popular locale for documentaries about wildlife and so forth, not to mention as a background for commercials, and Messrs Hobbes plied a regular and no doubt highly profitable trade with their makers.

I fell from grace a little when I explained that I was on my own and only wished to take a punt out for an hour or two, so muttered something about tight schedules, which went down well, and decided the atmosphere was now propitious enough for the big plunge.

"It's a bit of a lark, really," I explained. "You see, I was at school quite near here and we used to have punt races up to the bridge. A friend of mine, who was there at the same time, has had a bet with me. She said she could still do the distance faster than me, even though she's married now, with two children, and I bet her a magnum of champagne that she couldn't, so here I am to put it to the test."

"That right? Well, best of luck to you, say I. How about your friend, though? Hasn't she turned up?"

"Well no, unfortunately, she can't get away during the week, because of the children, you see, so she came last Saturday, when her husband was at home to look after them. You may remember her? Small . . . dark, rather unsmiling, as a rule, because she had a serious nature."

I did not add that she might have been wearing a head-scarf, feeling certain, if there was any foundation at all for my theory, that this was one article which would have been left at home.

Ms. Hobbes shook her head, clenching the cigarette between tight lips during this reckless manoeuvre.

"Not as I can call to mind. Saturday, you say?"

"Yes, early afternoon it would have been. Roughly

between two-thirty and four. I'm sorry you don't remember her because she told me she'd done the whole trip in an hour and twelve minutes, but she may have forgotten to wind up her watch, or perhaps it got wet. Anyway, it had stopped by the time she got home, so it could have been running down gradually and she said I'd better check out the exact time with you. You know, that you'd have a record of what time the punt went out and so on. . . ."

I tailed off, aware that the story was probably sounding feebler with every word, but perhaps she was accustomed to inhabitants of the theatrical world behaving in an imbecilic fashion, almost expected it of them, for she replied quite seriously:

"Then your friend doesn't know much about our business. We were rushed off our feet this time Saturday. They were queueing up halfway to the High Street. Not so many of them wanting punts these days, but you know what I mean?"

"All the same, I suppose you do keep records of how long each boat is out and so on?"

"Oh yes, we'd have to do that, wouldn't we? So we'd know what to charge for excess and that. And then there's the V.A.T. and all the rest of it. But we don't keep a note of names, or whether they went in a group or on their own, see? Wouldn't make any difference to the price, would it?"

"Yes, I do see that; and you don't happen to have noticed anyone who was alone, who might have been my friend?"

"Sorry, dear, can't say I do. Tell you what, though; I'll have a bit of a think while you're out and if anything clicks I'll let you know."

A party of people had come into the yard, carrying picnic baskets and fishing tackle, so I knew my time was up and allowed myself to be led away and handed over to a junior Hobbes, who was in charge of the embarkation arrangements. The time was then exactly twenty minutes to three which, by my reckoning, was the earliest that Vera could have started out on Saturday.

Forty minutes later I tied up by the Waterside

boathouse. Allowing for the fact that I was probably
slightly more expert with the paddle, I estimated that Vera
could still have reached the same point by three-thirty,
giving her a full hour, while Eddie and I were in the
theatre, to walk up the steps, through the narrow passage
past the kitchen to the art show, there to carry out her
business, before returning to the punt.

It was true that the upstream return journey would
have taken longer, how much longer still had to be verified,
but at all events I did not regard that as any impediment. If,
by ill-chance, Eddie had arrived back at the hotel ahead of
her, it would have been easy to explain that she had been
out for a stroll, hoping to clear her head and, furthermore,
the short walk from the river bank to the stables would not
have presented her with any serious hazards either. If she
had met anyone on the way, she had only to say, or allow it
to be assumed, that she was feeling better and was now on
her way to the theatre. No explanations of any kind would
have been needed for Hattie's benefit, since she would
doubtless have been unaware that Vera had ever left the
premises.

Unarmed with such plausible excuses of my own for
being found on them, I remained in the shadow of the
boathouse, playing out the required time by mentally
following Vera's progress and allowing her an interval of up
to ten minutes in which to conclude her business with
Hattie. The reconstruction was almost complete and had
become so vivid by this time that I half expected Vera to
come trotting down the steps in person at the appointed
moment, and so there was a special piquancy in the fact
that, slap on cue, a woman actually did materialise at the
top of them. The picture was slightly flawed, however,
because she was not Vera, but my ex-best friend, Tina
Blundell, who, as I soon realised, was behaving in a
somewhat outlandish fashion.

For a while she remained at the top of the steps, slowly
turning her head and casting her eyes around in a
painstaking inspection of her surroundings. Fortunately for
me, this did not involve so much as a flicker of a glance
towards the river, but was confined to ground level. The

operation appeared to be fruitless though, and she next turned her attention to the box hedge, which separated the steps from a rock garden, parting one or two of the branches and peering down into the gaps. Still no reward, and she then climbed over the hedge and extended the search to the rockery itself.

It was all quite mystifying and I longed to call out and ask what she was looking for, but unfortunately the essence of the expedition was to discover whether a punt could be moored on that spot for fifteen or twenty minutes, without exciting the attention of anyone at Waterside.

However, curiosity finally overcame discretion and I was telling myself that I could make an exception in Tina's case, since anyway I intended to give her a full account of the afternoon's excursion, when I saw that she had abandoned the search and was climbing diagonally away from me, up the bank and on to the levelled-out path at the top. A few seconds later she disappeared round the side of the house.

The boat hirer was in the act of lighting a fresh cigarette when I went into the office to settle my account and, as soon as it was firing away sufficiently to manage on its own, she inspected my ticket, saying:

"Let's see now! Yes, I make that one hour, thirty-five minutes. Have to charge you the full two hours, of course. Still, you won't mind that. How did it go?"

"Not so well as I'd hoped. I'm out of training."

"Shame! And no news about your friend, I'm sorry to say."

"Never mind. I'll just have to give her the benefit of the doubt and declare her the winner. I'm sure she made faster time than me, anyway. Lugging children in trolleys round the supermarket probably does wonders for keeping the arm muscles toned up."

"I asked Jim, my nephew, about it and, funnily enough, he does remember someone a bit like you described."

"You don't say?"

"Couldn't be her, though. Not unless she was cheating."

"Why's that?"

"She took a rowing boat. That's one reason why he remembered her. She'd got this camera, see, and she told him she just wanted to go a few hundred yards downstream till she found a spot where she could get some good pictures of the bridge, with the church in the background and all that. He thought she'd have been better off in a punt, instead of trying to do it rocking about in one of those rowing boats and anyway it was a daft thing to be doing on a Saturday, when you could hardly see the bridge with all that river traffic cluttering up the view. But he didn't say anything and it wasn't him brought her in when she got back, so that's not much help, is it? And it doesn't sound like it could have been your friend."

"No, it doesn't," I agreed, striving not to sound elated by the bad news. I had realised, naturally, that there were quicker ways of going by water than the one I had just put to the test, but had rejected the idea of a motor launch, on the grounds that in the quiet backwater where Waterside was situated the engine would have been audible from a quarter of a mile off and, although she could have glided in with the current, no such dodge could have been used for her departure. What I had completely overlooked, possibly because my own navigating experience had all been with the gentle, placid punt, was that an expert oarsman could probably have completed the round trip in approximately half the time it had taken me.

I might easily have kissed Ms. Hobbes, if her cigarette had not been in the way.

FIFTEEN

Considering a small contribution to the housekeeping to be now overdue, I called in at the butcher, greengrocer and wine merchant on my way back to Tina's flat and found her already at home when I staggered in with my load. She also had a visitor.

This was Sergeant Dexter, who had called to restore my property and, evidently determined to do so in person, had been given a cup of tea while he waited.

Very stiff and ill-at-ease they both looked too and, seeing them together like this, I was immediately struck by another resemblance. Each had the same gangly build, the same narrow face and sallow complexion, and even their pessimistic expressions were remarkably alike. It started up a brand-new and pleasing train of thought, for one of the happiest marriages of my acquaintance is between two people who could easily be mistaken for brother and sister. There was no denying that the weekend at Waterside was turning out to be more exciting and eventful every minute.

Unfortunately, there was also no denying that, given the diffidence of one of the parties and the prickly manners of the other, much spade work would be needed to make this path run smooth. So I accepted a cup of tea and then embarked on some reminiscences about the dear old days in Storhampton, when Robin and I were first married and he and the Sergeant had got to know each other. I kept trying to drag Tina into the conversation, though with singularly little success until, turning to her and saying: "That must have been the time when you were with that ballet company in Milan, wasn't it?" things began to look up.

"About then, I suppose," she replied.

I drank my tea in silence, then noticing that the teapot needed refilling, took it out to the kitchen, from whose fastness I heard the Sergeant clear his throat:

"I was lucky enough to get to La Scala several times in my salad days. Did you ever perform there?"

Poetic licence or not, they were off at last.

He did not stay above ten minutes after that, but the start had been made and I could leave it to future inspiration to contrive another accidental meeting. Meanwhile, there were other matters needing attention.

"Now it can be told," I said, removing 'Judgement Day' from its brown envelope. "What do you say to that?"

"Not bad. Pretty good of you, anyway."

"Do you notice anything?" I asked, ignoring this comment.

"Yes, of course I notice something. What a fatuous question. I notice three heads which, reading from the top, are Vera's, Eddie's and yours."

"I mean, anything apart from that?"

"Well, you've all got what might be called viewing aids floating about in front of you," she replied, studying the drawing with more care, "and obviously they're meant to describe the personalities of the subjects. Eddie's monocle, for instance; he doesn't actually use one, but it fits perfectly with the silly-ass type he projects. And you've got a magnifying-glass, which is rather a neat comment on your passion for subjecting everything and everyone to minute analytical scrutiny."

"I don't underestimate Hattie," I said, "and it wouldn't surprise me if she had hit on something a trifle more factual than that, the magnifying-glass being the conventional badge of the amateur detective, for instance. But you haven't mentioned the most important one yet."

"The most important one being Vera, I take it?"

"And what is that object dangling in front of her nose?"

"A miniature telescope, by the look of it. What's that supposed to signify? That she's a scientist, but only in a small way?"

"That wouldn't surprise me, but the point is, do you know another word for a tiny telescope?"

"Not offhand."

"Then I'll tell you. The word is 'spyglass'. I wasn't sure till I looked it up in the dictionary, but it's there all right. So what do you say to that?"

It was quite a triumph that for once I had succeeded in shaking her out of her mould of indifference, though also a relief that Sergeant Dexter was not present to see the terrible scowl which she turned on me. It would have spelt doom for all my romantic hopes.

"You mean," she said, speaking very slowly, "you actually mean to suggest that Hattie thought Vera was a spy?"

"Quite sure of it. What's more, she was probably right. In addition, I'd like you to know that Robin is half inclined to take the idea seriously too, which is mainly what encouraged me to plod on. That, plus the fact that I really liked Hattie and admired her work. She may have had her malicious streak, with a dash of kleptomania thrown in, according to one, but I excuse a few weaknesses of that sort in people of exceptional talent. Whereas the assumption that she would commit suicide just because she was too fat is simply insulting."

"Yes, okay, Tessa, but to get back to that other assumption, that Vera is a spy; if Robin does take it seriously, you must have something to back it up, but I do wish you'd explain how you arrived at such an extraordinary conclusion."

"By degrees, naturally, as one always does in such cases."

"But what first set you off on it?"

"I suppose there were several little piles of evidence building up and they all came together in a great big heap when Sergeant Dexter showed me the sketch of Vera with the spyglass. Isn't he attractive, by the way?"

"Is he? Can't say I noticed particularly. Do get on with it!"

"Well, here are some facts; not necessarily in the order I learnt them, but just the plain facts. The first being that Vera either is or, more likely, is posing as a refugee from behind the Iron Curtain."

"That sounds like half fact and half conjecture."

"Not entirely, because if you'd had the chance to observe her as I have, you'd know that posing is practically her métier. Another fact is that she went to the art exhibition before I did and therefore must have seen the 'Judgement Day' sketch and must have taken in the implications."

"Why must she?"

"It was very prominently displayed and something had definitely upset her because she came bounding back into the ante-room and started up a conversation about obesity, which Hattie very civilly responded to. Now, there's something wrong there, because if she was feeling well enough to sit down and chat with a girl she'd scarcely clapped eyes on before, how can she also, given her much vaunted sense of duty, have been too ill to take more than just a perfunctory glance at those pictures? You know yourself that most of them were Hattie's work and they were arresting, to say the least. Not the kind of things one could dismiss with a single glance, unless one had more pressing matters to deal with. So it's my belief that Vera realised Hattie has recognised her and was scared stiff that she'd pass on the news in less subtle terms than a drawing. However, her training would have taught her to use her wits to get out of tight corners and it's quite conceivable that she set things up by introducing the topic of compulsive eating and then promised to let Hattie have some miraculous slimming pills, which had done the trick for her. Am I going too fast for you?"

"No, thank you very much."

"Well, you'll remember that they found some slimming pills tucked away in her paint box, but neither Patsy nor anyone else had the remotest idea that she was in the habit of taking them, and I bet you even money she wasn't. She'd have thrown them away, as soon as she got the chance, only unfortunately she died before the chance came. However, all this is jumping ahead because we're still some way from the point where Vera handed over the pills."

"And in the meantime you haven't bothered to explain how Hattie happened to recognise Vera and also happened to know that she was a spy."

"Ah, but you see, another fact came my way this morning, relating to Hattie's father. He's a diplomat, as you know, and at various points in his career he's served in Russia, Poland and Czechoslovakia. Obviously, Hattie would have spent her school holidays wherever he happened to be, even if she hadn't been with him continuously, and, being Hattie, her eagle-eyes would have picked out and retained everything she saw. You'd agree that Vera has a most striking appearance, wouldn't you? And I dare say once seen by Hattie, never forgotten. But it's the circumstances in which she saw her that are important, and let's suppose that at the time Vera was working in some quite ordinary capacity, as a clerk or maybe interpreter in one of her own Government departments? Then five, six, maybe ten years later she turns up here as a persecuted refugee, with an English husband. She would obviously have dyed her hair and possibly had a bit of plastic surgery done on her nose, but no one can do much about their eyes, the way they're set and so on, and Vera's eyes are her most outstanding feature. No doubt, Hattie recognised her on sight, asked herself the inevitable question and came up with the logical answer. How's that?"

"All right, so far as it goes, I dare say," Tina replied grudgingly, "though goodness knows what information Vera could pick up which would be the slightest use to a foreign government."

"More than you think," I told her, "which is where Eddie comes in, and probably why she nabbed him in the first place. He's very susceptible, so he wouldn't have been a hard nut to crack."

"And what sort of access to top secrets is Eddie supposed to have, I'd like you to tell me."

"Oh, he gets around. He mentioned himself, in a jokey way, that he moves in high circles and it happens to be true. The fact is, he's about the most ancient and experienced sound broadcaster in the business. One of the few, incidentally, who have never moved over to television, so although his name is known to millions not many of them would recognise him. And he gets sent all over the world, you know, interviewing the biggest wigs there are; not to mention generals and cabinet ministers at home. When it's somebody really grand they always give the job to Eddie. So he's an old, familiar face and probably gets treated a bit like one of their own staff. I'm not suggesting that they strew secret information around like confetti, but just every now and then I expect a few crumbs come his way and a bagful of crumbs might add up to half a loaf."

"Which he then passes over to Vera to gobble up?"

"In the form of crumbs, naturally. She'd be the bread maker. She or her contact, or whatever they call them."

"Oh, you've found a contact for her too, have you? Aren't you thorough?"

"Well, she has to have one, you know, and it's not hard to guess who. This real or imaginary migraine certainly takes Vera through a lot of tricky situations. Eddie told me that she goes to a faith healer in the Cromwell Road and that he seems to be doing her good. Well, I ask you, Tina. Can you imagine a more ideal set-up for a spy? All sorts of strange people coming and going; no questions asked if one or two of them turn up regularly at the same time every week."

"So now you've got it neatly worked out, what's your next move?"

"I haven't decided yet. I'd hate to get Eddie into any trouble and yet it's hard to see how it could be avoided. Perhaps the best thing would be to wait for the inquest before I go any further. I was really just practising on you, testing for loopholes. If there were any I knew I could rely on you to pounce."

"That's good, because here comes one big enough to drive a coach and horses through."

"Ah!"

"Mind you, I could be wrong, but I presume your idea is that having discovered that Hattie was in possession of of this terrible secret, Vera made up her mind on the spot to murder her, dived into her bag and produced a bottle of poison labelled 'slimming pills'?"

"No, you shouldn't presume anything of the kind. I'm pretty sure the slimming pills will turn out to be harmless."

"So no connection there with Vera, after all?"

"On the contrary. What I think actually happened was this: Vera gave Hattie the bottle and urged her to take one, maybe two or three, and, while she was talking, removed the stopper and pretended to shake out the correct dose; but the poisoned pills had already been concealed in her palm and it was those which she actually handed over."

"And she just happened to be carrying this lethal dose around with her, on the principle that some such emergency might crop up any day of the week?"

"As far as the lethal dose goes, I shouldn't wonder at all. I am sure the well-dressed spy is never without the means of certain and instant suicide at hand. As for the harmless ones, she had only to call in at one of the multiple chemists in Gillsford, pick them up off the counter, along with various other everyday things like aspirins and so on, and pay as she went out. No itemised record of the transaction, no reason why the cashier should have remembered her or what she bought. And don't ask me how Vera could have made the journey back and forth to Gillsford with no car and without hiring a taxi, because I am now about to reveal the best bit of all."

"Strangely enough, however, Tina appeared to lose interest at this crucial point in the narrative and began looking at her watch in a furtive and anxious manner. The reason for this soon became clear.

"Well, it's nice that you've got it all buttoned up," she said, "and obviously you believe every word of it, but I'm afraid I can't stop to listen to any more just now. There's a film on which I've got to see and it starts in ten minutes."

"Why got to see?"

"It's about a dancer and Madam wants me to check it out for her. If it's suitable, she'll take some of her lot to see it tomorrow. They don't have classes on the last day of term and she thinks it will keep them out of mischief and give them something more wholesome to talk about. Do you want to come?"

I had half hoped that Sergeant Dexter, fired by his conversation with Tina and the new insight it had provided into the ballerina's life, might also have taken a whim to see this film, but, so far as I could tell in the few seconds before the lights went down, he was not present. And perhaps, after all, it was just as well, for he might have carried away a rather distorted picture. It was one of those perennial old fantasies about the conflict between love and career, and the heroine spent so much time glooming over it and arguing with her young man that it was hard to see how she managed to find much opportunity to practise. However, this proved to be no disadvantage at all because when the prima ballerina somewhat predictably fell down and injured her back this girl was unhesitatingly invited to take over her role. She did pretty well in it too, considering the lack of rehearsal; all of which made most people, including myself and the young man, extremely misty-eyed, but Tina's snorts and snarls of derision could be heard all over the cinema. Furthermore, she continued to nag me about the absurdity of it the whole way home and I was so flattened by this tirade that I completely forgot to ask her what she had been doing prowling about on the river bank and whether she had found what she was looking for. So I stood my framed photograph of Robin on its head, to remind me to do so in the morning.

SIXTEEN

(1)

The aide-mémoire was superfluous, however. For one thing, the mémoire managed perfectly well without it, Tina's strange cavortings being the first thing to hit me on waking. Secondly, when I got out of bed and sauntered through to the kitchen, it took less than a minute to discover that she had already gone out.

She had not left a note and, thinking that she might only have nipped up the road to fetch some milk or bread, I leant out of the sitting room window to try and see if her car was still parked on its regular spot. So far as I could tell, it was not, but as I was drawing my head in again a slightly more interesting sight presented itself. The white Rover, with Billy Bland at the wheel, drew up at the gate. Two stout women got out and walked up the path, as Billy drove off again.

There was nothing particularly mysterious about this, for I recognised the women on sight. They had both waited on us at the Waterside luncheon party, and during the brief periods when my attention was not fixed on more momentous affairs, I had amused myself by trying to guess whether they were sisters or mother and daughter, and whether Portuguese, Spanish or Italian. I now concluded that Billy had brought them over, probably as a matter of routine to clean out his surgery and consulting rooms, and that he preferred not to be there while they were doing it.

I soon found myself in sympathy with this prejudice because it was staggering how much noise they contrived to make as they went about their business and I wondered how it could be that, in a house of such solid contruction and separated from these toilers by three storeys, I could still hear them shouting at each other, in whatever language it was, over the sound of running water and the hum of the vacuum-cleaner.

The answer came two hours later, when I went downstairs on my way out to spend the day at Roakes Common. There had been no word from Tina and, growing bored at the prospect of waiting around for her indefinitely, or else mooning about Gillsford on my own, I had telephoned Toby and invited myself to lunch. The two women were still at it, although it was not the ground floor which was the scene of their operations, but the one below Tina's. The front door was wide open and the younger of the two was singing an old-fashioned ditty as she pushed the vacuum-cleaner up and down the hall. She grinned at me in a friendly way, then switched off the machine and went into a series of exaggerated gestures to illustrate her fatigue and exhaustion, puffing and blowing, fanning herself and going through the motions of mopping the sweat from her brow, having become conditioned, no doubt, to communicating largely in sign language.

"Too much work," she groaned, in case I had missed the point, and I made a bet with myself about the accent.

"Yes, indeed! Do you come from Portugal?"

"No, Spain. España."

"Ah! And I suppose you're getting the place ready for a new tenant?"

"Ten-hant?"

"Has the flat been let? Rented? Someone coming to live here?"

"Oh yes, two three days only, but still all this work."

"Must be hell. Do you know who it is?"

"Oh yes, very big man. Ambassador. Mrs. Bland say everything must be just so. You know?"

"Only too well. When is he coming?"

"Tonight. When we finish here we go back to Waterside. Afterwards we must come here again to prepare his dinner."

"Then I'd better not keep you. Sounds as though you'll have your work cut out."

She looked bewildered, so I made a scissors movement

with my fingers, turned it into a wave and continued on my way.

"So, presumably, Connie's idea was that it would be distressing for him to stay at Waterside, so close to the scene of his child's death, but at the same time he couldn't be put up at the hotel like an ordinary mortal and this was her solution. Really, she's a marvel, that woman. In good times and in bad, drunk or sober, she still thinks of everything."

"Why drunk or sober?" Toby asked.

"There's a popular theory in some quarters that her troubles are due to alcohol, and I suppose that might account for those mysterious black-outs and also for the fact that she appears to be living in a financial dream world."

"Does your friend, Tina, subscribe to this theory?"

"She flares up like a forest fire at the mere mention of it, which probably means she does. What really worries her, though, is not so much Connie hitting the bottle as my suggestion that Billy, so far from restraining her, is busily pouring out the drinks."

"So that eventually the poor lady will either kill herself or be tucked away in a home, leaving the field clear for the Madam of his dreams?"

"Exactly! And I don't think that, secretly, Tina would be averse to such an outcome, as it happens. She's on Madam's side, in so far as she disapproves of the snobbery and extravagance of the present regime. Waterside represents something special for her too, the place which gave her the first taste of happiness and fulfilment, and she's bent on preserving it, at all costs. The trouble with Tina, though, is that she's a bit of a Puritan, and I dare say what really makes her so sensitive on the subject is that, however desirable, the end doesn't justify the means. However, I haven't come here to bore you about all their troubles."

"Oh really? What have you come here to bore me about, then?"

"About Vera being a fraud, a spy and a murderess."

"Oh good! That sounds like a passable ten minutes' worth."

Thus encouraged, I gave him the full Vera saga, very much as I had reeled it off for Tina. I had been relying on him for a different response from hers and I was not disappointed.

"Splendid," he announced, having heard me through without interruption. "You are at the top of your form and I've no doubt you're absolutely right in every particular. The only snag is . . ."

"Yes?"

"It sounds to me as though it will be so pitifully easy to prove or disprove and, if you should turn out to be absolutely wrong in every particular, you will have such a very short run for your money. Surely it would be the work of a moment for Robin to find out whether Vera is a genuine refugee or not and, if she is, doesn't the whole theory come clattering to the ground?"

"Not at all," I said firmly. "You surely don't imagine that the spy manipulators leave such matters to chance? I have no doubt whatever that there was once a real Vera something or other, about the same age as our spurious one and similar to her in appearance. I expect she died in an asylum or prison camp, or something terrible, but they gave it out that she'd been released and then passed all her papers, birth certificate and so on, to Vera number two. I'll bet you anything that her documentation is impeccable."

"Oh, well done!" Toby said. "You've never been better!"

"Do you honestly think so?" I asked, gratification faintly shadowed with doubt in the face of such unqualified praise.

"I honestly do. You have my word."

"I'm pleased, of course, but you know, Toby, I do find it a little weird. I didn't expect you to be so contentious as Tina, but I was sure you'd find one or two flaws."

"Ah well, you see, I wouldn't want to do that, because everything you've said ties in so neatly with my own views."

"Seriously? You mean you'd already come to the same conclusion about Vera?"

"Not Vera, no, not at all. I've hardly given her a thought, except to notice in passing that she has an unfortunate tendency to exhibitionism, but I've known for years that Eddie was a spy."

"You're joking?"

"Certainly not. I don't wish to malign him in any way, but I should have said it was obvious."

"I must say, Toby, for someone who doesn't wish to malign someone, you're not doing particularly well. And I simply cannot go along with such an extraordinary idea. I've always suspected that Eddie was in the wrong business; I feel sure he could make a vast fortune doing commercials for British gin on American television. But a spy! And Eddie, of all people! It wouldn't have occurred to me in a million years. You can't possibly know any such thing."

"Well, when I say I know, perhaps that is a slight exaggeration. Let us say I have always assumed it to be so. It is really the only way one can explain him."

"Why is it? I don't understand you."

"Then consider the facts. He has an important and responsible job. In fact, you could say that he was at the very top of his own rather specialised profession. To have come so far in that cut-throat world you would need to be a tough and shrewd manipulator. Able to size people up, too, and handle awkward situations with the suave and tactful touch. You agree?"

"Yes, I'm not arguing about that. I still don't see why it makes him a spy."

"Then you're not trying very hard, because the man I've just described, the working Eddie, so to speak, must be the true one; clever, ambitious and sharp as a needle. Now, at what point does that description fit the Eddie we know and love?"

"Nowhere at all, but then I've always suspected that the silly-fool manner was a bit of a pose."

"Of course it's a pose; the most gigantic pose ever invented. It must be fifty years since that type of Englishman existed, if he ever did, and in case you're about to ask why he created such a fairy-tale, outdated character for

himself, I shall tell you. When you are leading the double
life and in constant fear of giving yourself away, you need to
cover your secret one with a thick layer of pretence and the
thicker it is the deeper your secret is buried. If you ever
permitted yourself to behave naturally you would be in
imminent danger of betraying yourself every time you
opened your mouth."

I told him that for all I knew he could be right, in
general terms, but that it did not follow that all *poseurs*
were spies. There could be dozens of other reasons for the
thick layer of pretence, and nothing would ever convince
me that this particular one applied to Eddie. Nevertheless,
I was more shaken by his argument than I cared to admit
and on the drive back to Gillsford I was struck by a memory
which depressed me still further.

One little incident which had occurred on the
morning after Hattie's death had never been properly
explained, nor slotted into the general scheme of things,
and I found myself reliving once more the moment when
Eddie and Vera came into the hotel lounge, where Robin
and Toby and I had just met, and heard again Eddie's
lighthearted voice asking whether it were true that a
Waterside girl had drowned herself.

I had not thought much about it at the time, having
been prepared for some such rumour to be gaining currency
before long, and it was not until much later, when we
realised how successful Connie Bland's hushing-up tactics
had been, that I became puzzled by the fact that Eddie, and
Eddie alone, had stumbled on this near-truth.

No doubt, Toby would have explained to me that it
was an instance of the real man peeping out from behind
his cover and that Eddie, being already aware of Hattie's
death for the very good reason that he had devised it, had
invented the rumour out of a compulsive need to discover
what developments had resulted.

However, I did not need Toby to spell all this out for
me and drove on to Queen Anne House in a state of deep
and utter gloom.

(2)

Tina's car was still not in evidence, its usual space now being occupied by a decrepit-looking Volkswagen, and when I opened the front door I found Pauline seated in the hall, looking every bit as despondent as I felt. She was clutching the handle of a trug which rested across her knees and, since it contained scissors, secateurs and other tools of the florist's trade, I concluded that she had been sent by her mother, perfectionist to the last, to arrange the ambassadorial flowers.

The toothy grin went into top gear when she saw me and she sprang up with such verve and alacrity that the trug tipped over, scattering its contents on to the moss green Wilton pile.

"Oh, blissikins, Tessa!" she gabbled, as I helped to pick them up. "I can't ever tell you how relieved I am to see you! You've saved the day!"

It was nice to know that I had brought some sunshine into her drab life, but the greeting was over-effusive, even by Pauline's standards, so I waited for the pill to emerge from all this jam. It did not take long.

"Could you be an absolute angel, Tessa, and let me into Tina's flat? I mean, you have got a key, haven't you? Oh Lord, please don't say you haven't."

"I won't because I have, but what do you want to get in there for?"

It was probably none of my business, but one fell so naturally into the habit of treating Pauline like a retarded imbecile and she never seemed to resent it.

"Well, you see, the thing is, Tessa, Mummy suddenly remembered that the ormolu clock in the flat which Sir Charles is going to use has gone to be repaired and it's left a horrid gap on the mantelpiece. So she wanted me to pop up to the top flat, when I came to do the flowers, and borrow the mahogany one from there. It's about the same size, you see, but the frightful thing is that I've come without the key and the great man might turn up at any moment. Mummy will simply skin me if I go back and report that I haven't been able to do it, so please be a darling and wave your magic wand."

"I can let you in easily enough," I told her. "No trouble at all. But hasn't it occurred to you that Tina may raise some objection to your mother commandeering part of her furnishings?"

"Good gracious no, of course she won't," Pauline replied, sounding as though this were the silliest question imaginable, which perhaps it was.

"What I still don't understand though," I said, pounding ahead of her up the first flight of stairs, "is why you didn't explain all this to Tina and ask to borrow her key?"

"Yes, I know, that's what I should have done, but it wasn't my fault, honour bright! I couldn't find her, you see. I searched absolutely everywhere and then someone told me that she'd left immediately after lunch and I was getting into a panic by then, because of the flowers and everything, and I just kept my fingers crossed that she'd be here. Only, she's not and I simply couldn't think what to do."

Pauline was quite breathless by this time, but at least she was partially vindicated as soon as we entered the flat. The note I had left propped up on the hall table that morning had been removed and another put in its place. The writing was tall and narrow and rather cramped, as befitted the author's physique, and the message was fairly typical too.

"Gone to Oxford. Private Class. May not be back till late. Stew ready to go in oven, if you want it. T."

It occurred to me in passing that one could almost believe that she was avoiding me, although since I had more or less forced myself on her perhaps this was excusable, if not altogether endearing. In any case, it was not the moment to dwell on personal wounds, for Pauline was fidgeting at my elbow in agonies of impatience, and, putting the letter down, I said:

"Okay, let's get started! Where does the clock live?

Above the fireplace and flanked by two shepherdesses, if memory serves."

"Yes, that's what Mummy said," Pauline muttered, darting into the sitting room. However, she advanced only a few feet towards her target before stopping dead in her tracks, as though she had been shot through the heart.

"My God!" she moaned in a voice of doom. "It's stopped!"

This was undoubtedly true, and simultaneously I realised that I had been subconsciously aware for some time that the hands were set permanently at twenty past four, although I could not recall whether this had always been so, or not.

"Keep calm," I said. "I expect she just forgot to wind it up. Now, where would the key be, I wonder."

It was not on the shelf, so I pulled open the tiny wooden door below the clock's face and instantly all was explained. There was a thick roll of white paper, with a rubber band round it, standing upright inside.

Using only the tips of a thumb and one finger, I carefully eased it out and then gave the pendulum a gentle tap. It swung into action immediately, settling into a regular beat and I closed the door again.

"There we are, Pauline! What could be simpler? Either the maddening tick tock got on Tina's nerves, or else she has seen this as the ideal place to keep her will."

"Oh, you are a lambie pie, Tessa," she said, all gush and simper again. "How would I ever have managed without you?"

"The key's in there too," I told her, "but if I were you, I wouldn't wind it up or tinker about with the hands until it's safe and ready in its new home. These old clocks can be temperamental and it might hit back if we push it around too mercilessly."

This advice brought on another flurry of anxiety and Pauline jumped backwards, as though taking my words literally:

"Oh Lord, Tessa, I feel awful asking you another favour, but you know what a clot I am. Things always seem to get gummed up as soon as I touch them and I have a ghastly feeling it will stop again if I carry it down myself. I suppose . . . ?"

"I don't mind lending a hand, if it's going to be that much of a worry to you," I informed her graciously, being curious to see this flat which Hattie's father was to occupy; and as soon as we had set the clock in place and satisfied ourselves that all was well with it, I wandered off on a tour of exploration. It was, as I had foreseen, an apartment of great luxury and taste and provided with everything man could desire, to delight the eye and save the labour.

"Will he be staying here on his own?" I asked Pauline, who was trailing along in my wake, obviously torn between fear of offending me and feverish impatience to get out before His Excellency caught us on the premises.

"No, he's bringing an A.D.C. or someone. Which reminds me, it might be a bright idea to . . . um . . . skedaddle before they turn up. Bit embarrassing, if they were to walk in, don't you think?"

"Oh, very well," I agreed, having seen all I wanted, "but there's still one thing you must do before you leave."

"Oh dear, is there? What have I forgotten now?"

"Your trug. You left it in Tina's flat."

All this climbing up and down stairs, fraught as it had been with nervous anxiety, had left her looking quite washed out and, since there was still some whisky left in Robin's bottle, I suggested that she should stay another five minutes and have a drink.

I half expected her to say that she would love a gingerpop, but in fact she accepted the whisky with great speed and alacrity, saying:

"Oh whoops, what fun! It's such a lark being with you, Tessa, but it mustn't be more than five, or Mummy will be wondering what on earth's become of me."

This struck me as a funny thing for a mummy to be wondering at six o'clock in the evening about a woman in her mid-thirties, and it then occurred to me that the well-known relationship between Pauline and Mrs. Bland might be largely mythical. Perhaps she had built up this image of

Connie as the domineering, demanding mother out of a desperate need to excuse her own inadequacy and lack of initiative; and also, perhaps, because it was preferable to admitting even to herself that what she actually suffered from was a yawning maternal indifference. It was a thought which for the first time brought stirrings of curiosity about Pauline as an individual and I attempted to draw her out a little.

"I suppose you've met him before?" I asked her. "What's he like?"

"Who?"

"Hattie's father."

"Oh well, yes I have, as a matter of fact. He used to put in an appearance occasionally when Hattie first came to us, but he hasn't been lately and he wouldn't know me from Adam."

"Why not? I'm sure Hattie must have talked to him about you."

"About me? Gracious no, I'm quite sure she wouldn't. She hardly knew I existed. Not many people do, actually.

"But I understood you were one of the few people who were able to get close enough to become quite friendly with her."

"Whoever told you that?"

"Someone . . . forget now."

"Well, it's not true, I'm sorry to say. I mean, just because. . . ."

"What?"

"Oh, when she first started going to art classes in Oxford I had the job of chaperoning her, so of course I got to know her just a little. But it only lasted for a term or two. After that she was considered to be old enough and sensible enough to go on her own. She wasn't the type to play hookey and spend the time at the flicks, worse luck!"

"Why worse luck?"

"Because I rather enjoyed those trips. Of course, Mummy used to give me masses of chores to do in Oxford and a huge shopping list to get through, but I didn't mind that. It was fun to break out of the routine for a bit and I was rather disappointed when it stopped. I supposed I must have grumbled to someone; but that was years ago and there was never anything personal between me and Hattie. We used to talk a bit on the journey and she seemed quite glad of my company, but all the same I bet she didn't give two hoots when I stopped going."

"So you wouldn't have got any clue as to why she might have been contemplating suicide?"

"Gosh no, none at all. She always seemed to be such a merry person. But I'd better not talk about it, if you don't mind, Tessa. Mummy has absolutely forbidden me to discuss it with anyone and she'd slay me if she found out. Anyway, I must run now, or I'll be in trouble. Bye bye and thanks ever so much for your help."

Run was the word for it and she was halfway to the front door before she'd got the last words out and, although I followed her into the hall, she had gone before I had time to point out that once again she was leaving without her trug. However, I did not bother to go after her, having more important matters on my mind just then. The sight of Tina's note, still propped against the Sunderland jug on the hall table, had set me wondering afresh whether she was deliberately avoiding me and, if so, why. This, in turn, brought back the memory of her odd behaviour on the river bank and I paced about the sitting room, picking things up and putting them down again, while cudgelling my brain to find some connection between these two puzzles.

The peregrination eventually brought me to the fireplace, where my eye lighted once more on the roll of paper which had been concealed inside the clock, and I feel sure, indeed could almost swear, that it was in a spirit of pure absent-mindedness that I slid off the rubber band and started to unroll it. Be that as it may, there was no absence of mind in the way in which, after a single glance, I opened it out fully and studied it in every tiny detail. It was a pen and ink drawing of birds, fish and animals, each with a human face attached to it, the very one, in fact, which Hattie had shown me when she was working on it.

SEVENTEEN

Her Britannic Majesty's ambassador, with A.D.C. in tow was delivered by Billy in the white Rover to his temporary lodgings soon after half past six. All three men entered the house and about five minutes later Tina's doorbell rang. Before going to answer it, I replaced the roll of paper in its rubber band and tucked it out of sight behind a cushion. The caller was Dr. Bland.

"Sorry to disturb you," he said, "but I gather Pauline left a basket here."

"Yes, she did. Do come in and I'll fetch it for you. Have you time for a drink?" I added when, instead of waiting in the hall, he followed me into the sitting room. "Do say yes, because I'm all on my own and getting terribly bored."

This was untrue because I had just spent a fascinating twenty minutes working away at fever pitch with pencil and paper and the job was far from completed. However, I no longer had much doubt that Tina was purposely keeping out of my way and reckoned myself safe from interruption by her for some time to come. Furthermore, Billy really appeared to be in need of a stimulant. He looked sad and jaded and appeared to have shrunk a little.

"Well, when you put it like that, Tessa, how can I refuse?"

"This one all right?" I asked, holding up the whisky bottle.

"The best there is. I'm sorry you've been left on your own like this."

"Oh well, can't be helped. Tina's kept pretty busy at the moment, what with private lessons and all."

"So she's managing to fit those in too, is she? I'm glad of that."

125

"It's where she is now."

He smiled at me, that endearing, almost conspiratorial smile, which seemed to be expressed mainly in his eyes:

"Well, not at this precise moment, as it happens."

"Oh?"

"No, she's over at The Lodge. Our poor old Patsy has had a collapse of sorts and Tina very kindly volunteered to supervise the girls' supper and bedtime. It was very good of her, but I must say I hadn't realised it would mean neglecting you like this. That was naughty of her. Pauline could have managed, I expect."

"It doesn't matter at all," I said.

"Forgive my saying so, but I rather think it does. Not to you, perhaps. I remember you as the sort of live-wire who never had much trouble finding something to occupy herself with, but I think it matters to Tina. She's a bad girl and I shall tell her so."

"Well, please don't quote me, will you? I'm not really feeling sorry for myself and it was very kind of her to put me up at all, just because I . . . had an urge to spend a few days here. I can't honestly expect her to disorganise her life on my account."

"No, but it might not be a bad thing, just the same. She's a sad, secretive little creature, in some ways; still caught in the chains of that unhappy childhood of hers, I often think. My wife and I quite worry about her. It's unwholesome at her age to devote so much time to work. That's why we were both pleased when we heard you were staying here. You're such a jolly, happy-go-lucky soul and we hoped you might shake her up a bit."

I can take any amount of compliments, as a rule, and come scampering back for more, but I was uncomfortably aware that this one was undeserved. Whatever my motives in planting myself on Tina, the laudable desire to act as a tonic to her spirits had certainly not been among them. So I chose this moment to offer him a refill, which being accepted gave me a chance to change the subject and ask whether there was anything seriously wrong with Patsy.

"Nothing you could put your finger on. She's getting

old, just like the rest of us, poor dear, and she's been under great strain these past few days. It's all been a little too much for her."

"She ought to think about retiring."

"Patsy retire? Oh, I hope not. We'd be lost without her. No, she'll pull out of it, once she's had a bit of peace and quiet, without all those chattering girls around."

"How is Mrs. Bland bearing up, by the way."

"Oh, splendidly! But she can take any amount of knocks and still come up fighting."

"Yes, I know, she's wonderful, but all the same she didn't seem to be quite her usual self on the day of the drama competition. . . . When I had lunch with you?" I suggested, treading warily.

"Ah yes, of course," he said, not smiling now, but still sounding serene and composed. "I'd forgotten you were a witness to one of those little setbacks. And so naturally you've been wondering about it, haven't you? Well, let me assure you, Tessa, there's nothing wrong with Connie which couldn't be righted if she would only stick to a proper routine with the pills and injections."

I was at a loss to know how to respond to this, so assumed a polite, enquiring expression, as of one hoping to hear more, which this one certainly did, and he said:

"She has diabetes, you see."

"Diabetes?" I echoed in a stunned voice, my mind in a veritable whirl.

"No need to sound so shocked. It's not the end of the world. In fact, it's a fairly common complaint and perfectly easy to control, provided a certain regime is observed."

"The reason for my surprise," I said, pulling myself together, "is that Mrs. Bland is the last person I would expect to find neglecting herself in that way. I always remember her as being particularly down to earth and practical."

"Well, that raises an interesting psychological question, doesn't 'it? You're right, of course; her reactions haven't been at all what one would have foreseen, but I'm afraid the answer is that she hasn't yet managed to come to terms with her situation. Won't accept it, in other words. Up till now, she's scarcely had a day's illness in her life and she hasn't much patience with invalids. We all have our Achilles heel, don't we? I'm afraid this is hers. She refuses to admit that she has a chronic condition and therefore she doesn't always take the necessary steps to keep it in check. In fact, you could almost believe sometimes that she goes to great lengths not to do so."

"I don't understand," I said, although beginning to.

"I could give you a dozen examples, but to take only one: wine is very much a taboo in her case, and she hardly touches it, as a matter of fact, but I'd soon be in the doghouse if I didn't go through the motions of filling her glass, along with all the others. Everything has to be seen to be perfectly normal."

"I am sorry," I said. "I had no idea, and it must make life very complicated for you."

"You could say that, I suppose, but at least she may be lucky to have a doctor in the house; not to mention Patsy, who does far more than her share. Between us, we shan't allow her to go very far astray, you can be sure of that."

He swallowed the rest of his drink and stood up:

"Well, I've enjoyed our talk, Tessa. You always were one of the bright ones. I can say that now, without being accused of favouritism or worse, can't I? You know us all so well, without being emotionally involved, which makes it refreshing. And I know I don't have to hand out any pompous warnings about what I've told you being strictly confidential. Constance has an absolute horror of anyone, most of all the girls, learning about her complaint. God knows why, but she seems to feel that a weakness of that kind would somehow undermine her."

Which was one way, I reflected as I saw him to the door, of issuing a pompous warning, while disclaiming any such intention.

EIGHTEEN

"I suppose you noticed your clock had gone?" I asked, over a steaming mug of coffee the next morning.

I had been in bed when Tina eventually came home and, although still wide awake, had decided to give myself a night's sleep before tackling her.

"I was prepared for it," she replied calmly, adding in the same offhand tone, "Can't think why they bothered though. It doesn't go."

"Probably for aesthetic reasons; to fill the yawning gap between the two bronzes. Who prepared you for it?"

"Connie, of course. I suppose even she wouldn't consider it quite ethical to send Pauline barging in here to snatch up whatever she wanted, without offering some explanation."

"But you didn't speak to Pauline after the deed was done?"

"Didn't see her. I had to go and give a hand at The Lodge. Patsy was on the verge of a breakdown and couldn't cope."

"So I heard. Was she any better when you left?"

Tina's expression darkened and she slowly lowered her arm and placed her mug on the kitchen table:

"You seem to know an awful lot. How did you hear about the clock anyway?"

"I was here when Pauline came for it."

"You were, were you?"

"I've just said so. And how else would she have got in?"

There was a distinct pause before she answered and when she did it was plain that the bravado was becoming a little frayed at the edges.

129

"I didn't give it a thought. I'm quite sure Connie has keys to all these flats. I simply assumed she had given one to Pauline. It may not be very pleasant to know that they can come bursting in whenever they feel like it, but that's the price I have to pay."

"Then you may be relieved to hear that Pauline doesn't view it in quite the same light. When her mother sent her on this errand, her immediate reaction was to explain matters to you and get your permission. She couldn't find you though. I dare say you really were at a private class at that point, but Pauline, who has an uncomplicated brain, assumed that if you weren't at school you must be at home. Only, unfortunately, you weren't."

"But you were?"

"Yes."

"And, not having an uncomplicated brain, you couldn't rest until you'd found out why the clock had stopped?"

"Correct. If you'd been here, you'd have been able to fob her off easily enough. Found another clock or ornament; and if you had let me into your little secret I'd have done the same. Still, no use wailing about wasted chances now. The sketch is quite safe, by the way. It's in the left-hand drawer of the desk and no one but me has seen it."

"So now I suppose you are waiting to be told why I lied to you and pretended I hadn't been able to find it?"

"No, I'm not."

"You're not?"

"No, because I'm pretty sure I already know. So you needn't bother. Are you going to the inquest, by the way? It's at twelve, isn't it?"

"What? Oh, is it? I don't know . . . Listen, Tessa . . ."

"I said don't bother."

"Then kindly stop saying it, will you? Obviously, we can't leave it like this. What is it you know, or think you know?"

"I've had plenty of time to study the picture since it turned up so opportunely and it wouldn't take a genius to understand why you pinched it and then pretended it didn't exist. I still don't quite understand why, having brought it back here to study at leisure, you hid it in the clock instead of destroying it, but perhaps it was simply because paper of that thickness is not so easy to dispose of in a flat. Too bulky for the lavatory and bound to give rise to awkward questions if you started lighting fires in a heatwave."

"No, that wasn't the reason," Tina said. "Go on!"

"I am also fairly certain I know what you were looking for in the vicinity of the boathouse, between three and four p.m. on the afternoon of Monday, 29th June," I continued, facetiously adopting the pompous drone of a stage constable.

Whether it was this that did it, or the remark itself, was not clear, but it was as well that her mug was almost empty, otherwise the contents must have splashed all over her furious, incredulous face, so fiercely did she slam it down on the table.

"It can't be true, Tessa? I won't believe it."

"You have to believe it. How else would I have seen you there?"

"Someone told you . . . no, you're right, I have to believe it. I caught sight of the punt too, at one point, I remember that now, but I never dreamt there was anyone in it. I took it for one of ours, which had been left out by mistake. Well, go on! You may as well finish, now you've started. What was I looking for?"

"It is my guess," I told her, "that there came a point when you recollected your own words, while telling me about Hattie's work routine. You said, you will remember, that she always made several sketches of everything she did and invariably kept every one of them."

"I remember."

"But then it struck you that you had only found that single drawing of the animals and fish, the one you had brought home and later hidden in the clock. So you began to wonder whether in fact there had been others and what had become of them. Am I right?"

"Go on!"

"Do I really need to? I should have thought it was obvious. I'd told you exactly where Hattie was when I came across her at work on this drawing, and you thought there was just a chance that she had left a rough sketch behind, that it could have dropped out of her portfolio, where anyone might find it and recognise one of the characters. So long as you couldn't rule out that chance, you felt compelled to go and look."

This time when I paused Tina did not command me to go on, but sat with her arms propped on the table, staring down into her mug. Then, without warning, she jerked her chair back and went over to the stove to switch on the electric coffee-pot.

"So you know it all, do you?" she asked, with her back to me. "I don't have to fill in any last detail?"

"No, it's all clear to me now. As I explained to you before, when I first saw the picture I hadn't set eyes on any of the Waterside gang for years. There'd been some changes, naturally, and my own memories were pretty hazy too. I remembered people more by quirks of character than by appearance. Patsy, for instance, was immediately associated in my mind with the squirrel and its pile of nuts; whereas I can see now that the face is nothing like hers. And then there was the cat on the ladder. That fits Madam all right, I thought to myself as soon as I met her, but no; wrong again. The features there belong to Belinda Jameson, depicted as leaping up the ladder of success, no doubt. Poor Madam actually appears as the hyena, which is not very kind, but one had the impression that Hattie didn't particularly care for her. There is just one thing you can tell me though, Tina. How long have you been aware that Connie had diabetes?"

"Oh . . . six, seven months."

"Patsy told you, I suppose?"

"Yes, and swore me to secrecy, which I had no intention of breaking."

"Which is why you played along so prettily with the neat little theory of alchoholism? Why, in fact, after your first fine fury had cooled and you'd begun to think straight, you actually encouraged me in it and helped to build it up? You knew it couldn't do much harm and it suited you to let me go bumbling along this false trail, confident that it would put me right off the scent?"

"That's about it."

"You're very clever," I told her, "and the galling thing is that you'd probably have succeeded, if it hadn't been for the accident of Pauline leaving her trug behind, which led to my little chat with Billy."

"Who told you that Connie was diabetic?"

"Also swearing me to secrecy, in his own special way, although he didn't extract any promises; probably saw no need for them. No doubt, he expected I'd be leaving here in a few days and that it might be years before I dropped in again. Also, not having seen Hattie's picture, he didn't realise just how much he was telling me. But I had been looking at it before he came and as soon as he mentioned diabetes I had the key. I knew then exactly what species of bird that was in the top left-hand corner and why it was raining down syringes and little bottles from its bow, instead of arrows. And so, of course, did you."

"Although I doubt if that would have been enough, on its own. I knew that she had quite a hand in Connie's treatment and medication and I'd had some nasty doubts for some time . . ."

"That Patsy, dear, reliable, kind old Patsy, was switching antihistamine or whatever for the insulin tablets and putting water in the hypodermic?"

"Something on those lines."

"Why? I mean, if it wasn't the picture that put the idea into your head, what did?"

"Two quite small incidents, really. There was one occasion when I caught her off guard. I'd gone in to ask her something, I forget now, and she was standing by the window, apparently pasting a label on to a bottle of pills. I did knock, but she can't have heard me, because I've never seen anyone so flustered and horrified as when she looked up and saw me watching her. All the same, I probably wouldn't have given it another thought if she hadn't torn fifteen strips off me for bursting in without permission. And that's so unlike Patsy, isn't it? The nearest she can usually get to a reprimand is to tell you you're a bad girl and then give you a peppermint cream to take the sting off."

"What was the other incident?"

"Even more negative. In fact, it was the lack of incident which chiefly worried me. You see, the point about Patsy, in this connection, is that she lives permanently at The Lodge. It's her home and so, to some extent, her routine doesn't vary from holidays to term. So far as the Blands are concerned, she's always on hand. But there was one occasion, right at the beginning of this term, when she had to go into hospital for a few days. Only a very minor operation, but it shook her badly, and when she came out Billy, who's always thoughtful and kind, insisted on her taking a proper rest. He issued instructions to all the rest of us to wait on her hand and foot and see that she didn't stir from her room. So, one way and another, she was out of action for over a week."

"In the course of which Connie was as bright as a button and never had a single setback?"

"That more or less sums it up," Tina admitted. "It may have been coincidence; I tried to persuade myself it was, but I never wholly succeeded."

"I wonder if withholding treatment from someone who needs it rates as murder?"

"Not unless someone dies."

"Yes, you're right. I keep forgetting that we've got the wrong corpse. You see where it leads us, though?"

"Oh no, you don't," Tina shouted, turning angry again all at once. "I've been waiting for this and I knew you'd get around to it sooner or later."

"Waiting for what?"

"The moment when you start accusing Patsy of Hattie's murder and I'm not having it, do you hear me, Tessa? There's simply no connection at all."

"You can't prove that."

"Oh yes, I can. The proof is lying in that desk drawer, where you put it. I've told you over and over again that if someone had killed Hattie to prevent her passing on some damaging information, then the murderer would have lost no time in destroying the evidence. Patsy had every opportunity to do so, but she handed over the drawing with all the others."

"Did she actually see you take it?"

"No . . . I . . . that is, she wasn't in the room the whole time. There was some confusion about one of the girls' trunks and she had to go and sort it out."

"So she could have torn up all the preliminary sketches and overlooked this one? After all, we've established that it was unusual for Hattie to make only one, so it's a contingency you can't rule out."

"Yes, I can and I rule it out absolutely. Patsy may have gone slightly bonkers on the subject of Connie and the way she runs the place; she's had provocation, heaven knows. She may even have persuaded herself that God in his wisdom has called Connie's number and shouldn't be opposed. But actually to murder someone, one of her own girls, is a very different matter. She's the gentlest, most soft-hearted woman ever born and the first person in my whole life to show me genuine kindness and affection, and I'm not having her called a murderess, so that's flat."

"Okay," I agreed.

"Besides," she went on less truculently, and somewhat shaken by my easy capitulation, "you have to face the fact that she's either a cruel, cunning murderer, who kills to save her own skin, or else she's a doddering old fool, who hasn't even got the wits to destroy the evidence which could convict her, but hands it over on request. You can't have it both ways."

"I've said okay, haven't I? No need to go on about it. But listen, Tina, what in fact do you intend to do? Patsy may only be a misguided old halfwit and you may have deep-rooted sentimental feelings towards her, but you still have to face the unpleasant facts. Or do you mean to sit tight and let it ride until one day Connie just slips into a coma and never comes out of it?"

"No, of course not, I'm not as barmy as all that, but no

action needs to be taken just yet. Patsy's in a state of
collapse, as you know, and she can't do any harm while
she's confined to her own quarters."

"And after that?"

"It may still be unnecessary. She's had a bad shock,
you know. I realise it was Hattie's death which caused it,
but it may have brought her up sharp and given her a new
slant on her own behavior. I'm hoping so, anyway."

"I hope so too."

"No need to be sneery. I'm not relying on that alone.
The Blands always go to their house in France as soon as
the summer term ends. If Connie comes home in fighting
trim, after a month or two there, and then things start
going wrong again, we shall know for certain who's to
blame and I shall confront her with it. That's why I kept
the drawing. If she denies it, I shall point to herself as "The
Sparrow, with My Bow and Arrow," to prove I'm not the
only one who'd discovered what she was up to. I should
think that would scare her pretty effectively."

"Yes, I should think it might. Unless, of course, it
proves so effective that she retaliates by sprinkling arsenic
on your cornflakes. So that's why you kept the drawing?"

"Yes, nothing to do with its being difficult to get rid of.
I could have dumped it in the school incinerator, nothing
easier. I suppose the clock was a silly hiding place, but it
was only intended as a temporary one. I was looking round
for somewhere suitable, where you . . ."

"Wouldn't be likely to go snooping around, in my
unorthodox fashion?"

"Precisely. It was the afternoon you went on the river
and I was standing with the damn thing in my hand,
wondering where to put it, when your friend, the Sergeant,
came to call. So I shoved it inside the clock before I went to
let him in. I nearly died when I realised he meant to sit it
out until you got back because, knowing you, I felt certain
the first thing you'd say when you walked in was that the
clock had stopped. But you didn't."

"Mechanical objects don't rivet me so much as people.
All my attention was on you and Sergeant Dexter and the

charming picture you made, chatting away so merrily over the teacups."

"Thank you so much; but the fact remains that you didn't notice it, neither then nor after we got back from the cinema. So it seemed as good a place as any and I left it there."

"Well, we appear to have cleared up a few mysteries and misunderstandings," I told her, "but the big puzzle still remains."

"What's that?"

"Who did kill Hattie?"

"And what became of your lovely theory about Vera being the Mata Hari of the Cromwell Road?"

"Still very much alive, but it's turning out to be more complicated than I had thought. To be honest with you, I am torn between conflicting loyalties. Perhaps it would be best to wait for the inquest before taking the next step."

"Then let's hope no more steps will be needed," Tina said. "Personally, I'm hoping for a verdict of suicide, with all the trimmings, and then we can try and put the whole rotten business behind us."

"Some with more success than others," I remarked.

NINETEEN

(1)

Tina's hopes were amply fulfilled and her cup must have been running over, for the verdict was Death by Misadventure. Perhaps this was inevitable since, in the absence of Vera, there was no one to testify that Hattie had been in any way depressed or out of sorts, still less that she had reason to be. Moreover, coroners are probably no more immune than most people from a reluctance to tread too heavily on the toes of the mighty. Mrs. Bland was rather mighty, in her own way, Charles McGrath, K.C.M.G., even more so.

Apart from formally identifying the remains as those of his daughter and of receiving the sympathy of the court, he was not required to take any active part in the proceedings, but during the brief period when attention was focused on him he established himself as a highly dignified and imposing personage. I was interested to notice too that his mouth, although tending that way, was not so small and mean, nor the squint nearly so pronounced as Hattie had depicted them, confirming my view that there had been little mercy in her keen, perceptive eye. However, I still considered it wrong that she should have been killed for it and said as much to Robin when I returned to London that evening.

"So you're not giving up?" he asked. "Coroners and juries may do their worst, but you go on regardless?"

"Certainly, so far as my opinions are concerned; though, as for giving up, I'm not so confident. My hands are tied and I don't see how even you could help to untie them."

"That's bad! Are you sure?"

"Well, I doubt if Scotland Yard would put two men on to trailing Vera day and night for an unlimited period, simply on the grounds that I believe she might be a spy, do you?"

"So Vera remains the number one suspect?"

"Yes, although I haven't ruled out Madam and I'm a long way from ruling out Patsy, whatever Tina may say. The trouble is that it would be just as hard to get positive evidence of their guilt as of Vera's. I scarcely know Madam and our relationship so far hasn't been quite cordial enough to invite her out for lunch and a nice long chat about hyenas and dolphins. And Patsy is equally inaccessible just now. The minute I showed my face in Waterside Tina would guess what I was up to and she'd throw a cordon round Patsy which would take me months to hack through."

"I can see how frustrated you must feel."

"And that's not the worst of it, Robin. The real

problem is that I haven't much enthusiasm for embarking on a programme which would harm and upset the Blands and I'd simply hate to have it proved that Patsy were guilty."

"But at least there are no conflicts of that kind with Vera?"

"Not Vera for herself, no, but the trouble there is that, although I'm pretty sure Toby was pulling my leg when he said that, if Vera is a spy, Eddie must be in the game too, I'm stuck with the idea now and I simply don't want to know."

"Don't tell me you're becoming squeamish?"

"No, my motives are purely selfish. I've always looked on Eddie as a truly good and kind man and I'd hate it to be otherwise. In some odd way, I feel it would be as diminishing for me as for him, if that doesn't sound pompous?"

"No, but don't be too depressed. Convictions are not necessarily less admirable for being misguided or different from our own."

"I know that, but it would still mean that he had been deceiving everyone all these years and that's the horrid part. He would still be a fake."

"So it's deadlock, is it?"

"Looks like it. No choice but to retire from the fray and admit defeat; and I don't much care for that either. Specially when you remember that poor Hattie was only seventeen and all she'd done was tell the truth, in her own peculiar fashion."

"Never mind," Robin said. "I'm sure something else will soon turn up to divert your mind from all this. You might even land that part in the serial your agent has been angling for. In the meantime, I'll take you out to dinner, somewhere very posh, and you can quiz the waiter about the ingredients of all the sauces and forget your troubles for one evening."

Perhaps this lighthearted dismissal of the problem was all the spur I needed, for, paradoxically, the next morning found me just as keen as ever to dig out the truth and, before I had even begun to consider ways and means, an opening of sorts presented itself.

I was looking down the end page of my diary, which is reserved for ex-directory telephone numbers, when my eye was caught by the last entry of all, which was Belinda Jameson's. Tina had given it to me before I left Gillsford and had also explained that after the bankruptcy and death of her husband Mrs. Jameson had become so sickened by all the people who rang up claiming to be journalists or creditors that when she moved to new and cheaper premises she had not had the number listed.

So, after I had done a little work on my agent, which consisted of coercing her into doing a little extra-mural work for me, I rang Mrs. Jameson's number. She answered herself and, having told me that Belinda had gone out for an hour or two, suggested I should leave a message.

So I identified myself and explained about having been a judge at the drama competition, adding that I had some information which Belinda might find useful, but that since I would prefer to obtain her own approval before passing it on, would like to call on her right away.

I think I must have begun to sound dangerously like a journalist or creditor by this time, because she became evasive, saying that she was sorry, but . . . oh well . . . yes, she supposed it would be all right, but the place was in an awful mess and she had to go out herself fairly soon. I promised not to take up more than ten minutes of her time and rang off before she could change her mind.

(2)

The place certainly was in an awful mess, although Mrs. Jameson could hardly be blamed for that. It was a small maisonette above a greengrocer's shop off the Edgware Road, cramped and shabby, with a strong smell of cabbage permeating every corner, which was probably endemic during the summer, when windows were open; but the worst mess of all had been created by Belinda's recent homecoming. Her trunk, half unpacked and with clothes, records and books spilling out of it, half filled the tiny hall, nearly all the remaining space being cluttered up by half a dozen carrier bags, so crammed with miscellaneous objects that some had literally burst at the seams.

It reminded me so vividly of my own arrival home at the end of my last term at Waterside and of the less than ecstatic expression on my mother's face when her beloved, with all her possessions, had been restored to her for the foreseeable future.

"You must be a very indulgent parent," I remarked, as we threaded our way through this mountainous rag-bag to the tiny sitting room. "My mother would have had several fits if I'd gone gallivanting off and left her with this lot to cope with."

Visualising her in my mind, as one does with people one has spoken to, but never met, I had created a picture of a rather faded middle-aged woman, prematurely aged by life's blows and buffets, but in no way at all did Mrs. Jameson measure up to this pathetic image. She was rather bold-looking, with extremely well-cut platinum-coloured hair and, even allowing for the fact that she had had half an hour to prepare herself, her clothes and make-up were of a startlingly high order. She also looked years younger than I had expected and I put her down as good-natured and rather stupid, a verdict which was not amended by a glance at the title on the paperback novel which lay open and face downward on the arm of a chair.

"It's not Belinda I blame, it's that old Mrs. Patterson," she said. "When you think of the fuss there used to be about their luggage at the beginning of term, all those lists of things to take back, half of them unnecessary and never worn, and then three months later they come back in this state. Disgusting, really."

"They're a bit upset there at present," I told her. "They've had some trouble, as you've probably gathered."

"Yes, I know, that's why they came home early. One of the girls committed suicide, didn't she? Not very nice, is it?

I'm beginning to think it's not altogether a bad thing Lindy won't be going back there."

"The Coroner gave it as death by misadventure."

"Oh, I know. I saw that in the paper this morning, but Lindy said it was just eyewash. All the girls knew she'd done it purposely and they weren't all that surprised either. Would you care for some tea, by the way? I never touch the stuff myself, but I can soon rustle up some, if you'd like it?"

"No, thanks awfully. I'm interested to hear you say they weren't surprised. I only met her once or twice, but she struck me as a very cheerful type."

"Really? Well, Lindy says she never could make out what she was doing at Waterside at all. She couldn't act and she couldn't sing or dance and her parents didn't seem to bother themselves much about her, so she must have felt a bit of a misfit, poor thing. Not like my old Lindy. She was always very popular and she walked off with all the prizes."

"Yes, I know, I've been meaning to congratulate you. She's very gifted."

"Thanks. It's nice to hear that, specially from a pro. And she's not gallivanting, by the way, she's gone after a job. Which reminds me: if you've something to tell me which you don't want her to hear, perhaps we ought to get started? She could be back any time now."

"Strangely enough, a job is exactly what I've come about."

"There now! I had a feeling it might be something of the kind."

"That was why it was essential to see you as soon as possible. They're auditioning at Her Majesty's tomorrow for a big new American musical. It opens with the original Broadway cast, so it's only for understudies, unfortunately, but if it runs they'll change the cast and there are several juvenile parts, so it might lead to something really good."

"Well, it's certainly kind of you to go to all this trouble, but the thing is, you see . . ."

"I've done a bit more than that," I said, all eagerness to get the full Lady Bountiful story out before her daughter returned. "I've made a deal with my agent and she's perfectly willing to give Belinda a letter of introduction, on my recommendation. She wouldn't expect commission, or anything like that."

"Well, as I say, it's very kind of you, and I know she'll be grateful and all that, but . . ."

It was dawning on me that this was not quite the rapturous reception I had been anticipating and I said less confidently:

"Of course, if this interview she's gone for now is going to lead to something better . . . ?"

"Goodness, no, it's nothing like that at all. She just wants to raise some cash, you see, and all the big stores start their summer sales next week. They don't all come on at the same time though, so if you're lucky you can move from one to another and be in work for the whole month."

I was appalled to hear this, for a friend of mine had once worked as a sales assistant during the peak Christmas period and she had told me that after three days of it she was near to collapse. I began to realise how justified Madam and Co. were in their opposition to Connie and why they had become so despairing under her rule.

"Forgive my saying so, Mrs. Jameson, but wouldn't it be a good idea for her at least to have a shot at this audition? It would be much more in her line than working in a shop and, if she did get taken on, the salary would be better too. There's always the remote chance that it might flop, but she'd still be getting experience and, with any luck, it could run for months, or even years."

"Yes, well, that's the snag, you see."

"Oh, is it? Why?"

"Please don't think I'm carping because I appreciate what you're trying to do, but if she did get a part in this musical, they wouldn't want her to drop out after six or seven weeks, would they? I mean, there wouldn't be any chance that they'd engage her on that basis?"

"No chance at all. The initial contract would most likely be for a minimum of six months."

"Yes, well, that's what you'd call the snag. You see, what Lindy's got in mind is five or six weeks' holiday job.

She doesn't care what it is, so long as she can raise some cash and so long as it's temporary."

"And then what?" I asked, thoroughly bemused.

"And then she's going to try for one of these music and drama schools. This Madam person has so dinned it into her that she needs at least another year's training that she's dead set on the idea now. That's why she needs the extra money; for the fees."

I was so shocked by this revelation that I barely paused to consider my words:

"But that's awful, Mrs. Jameson, really awful! I mean, I do realise that things have been rather hard for you both lately. Well, when one spends three or four days at Waterside, as I just have, one can't avoid picking up stray bits of news and gossip, but I really had no idea the situation was as bad as that."

"No need to be upset about it, my dear. We manage all right, on the whole. I've got a fairly decent part-time job and a small income of my own I managed to save from the wreck. We'll be able to rub along until Lindy starts earning. It's just these extras that we can't stretch to."

"I'm not quite with you," I said, this being an understatement. "You seem to be saying that things haven't got any worse for you and yet at the same time it's necessary for her to slog away like this to earn some money. I realise it's none of my business, but I shouldn't have thought that the expenses of a London school, when she'll be living at home, would be anything like the fees you've been paying up till now. They would probably barely cover the Waterside extras."

"You're right," Mrs. Jameson said, getting up from her chair and moving to the window. "They wouldn't be anything at all like I've been paying up to now."

Matters were becoming more mystifying by the minute, for she then proceeded to behave in a most peculiar fashion. First she leant out of the window, turning her head to left and right and then, evidently satisfied with her panoramic view of the street, went into the hall and stumbled through the clutter to the front door. I saw her open it and stand listening intently for a few seconds, before closing it again, returning to her chair and sitting down.

"Sorry about that," she explained, "but I had to make sure Lindy wasn't on her way in. It wouldn't do for her to overhear this. She's terribly sensitive on the subject, poor kid. It's not that she minds being hard up. In fact, sometimes I think she gets quite a kick out of it. You know, winning through and coming out on top, in spite of it. And she doesn't mind accepting all those nice presents from the other girls either. She sees that as all in the line of friendship and she's sometimes able to give them little things in return, which makes it all right. What she can't stand, has a real old phobia about, is anything she sees as charity."

"What do you mean by charity?" I asked. "Surely she wouldn't class my small offer in that category?"

"Oh, good heavens no, my dear. I wasn't referring to you. It was about the school fees. You see, for the last three years, ever since my husband died, I haven't paid a single penny; not for the fees nor the extras either."

"Oh, I see," I said untruthfully. "There was some kind of charitable trust who . . ."

"No, there wasn't; not unless you'd call Mrs. Bland a charitable trust, which could be one way of looking at it, I suppose. Doling it out to the starving orphans on her own terms, sort of thing. No, to be fair, she's been very good, in her way. When my husband died I told her I couldn't afford to keep Lindy on there any more and she wrote back saying there was no reason why the child should suffer for something that wasn't her fault and she'd be willing to waive the fees until I was back on my feet."

"That wasn't bad!"

"No, you're right. In fact, at the time I was over the moon. She even said she'd had such good reports of Lindy's work that she knew she'd turn out to be a credit to the school, so I mustn't think the debt was all on my side. I thought that was really good of her. I'd have walked barefoot across the Sahara at that point, if she'd asked me to."

"But since then?"

"I've learnt that there are other ways of paying besides money. It turned into charity, after all, and she seemed to think it gave her the right to dictate to me on every subject under the sun. I was giving Lindy too much pocket money; some of her clothes were unsuitable; she oughtn't to wear all that make-up. On and on, you name it! And it didn't stop there either. She started interfering in things right outside her sphere. Only a week or two back I got this long screed saying I ought to give more supervision to Lindy during the holidays, that she knew it was hard for me, having to go out to work and so on, but I must try and exert more control. Damn cheek, really, and I felt like telling her to go to hell and mind her own business."

"But you didn't?"

"No, when I'd cooled off a bit, I could see that Lindy would be the one to suffer, although I might just as well have, as it's turned out. Soon afterwards I got another letter, saying her accountants were making her cut down expenses and Lindy would have to go. Not quite as bald as that, but it's what it amounted to and it's left me in a right old fix. Personally, I agree with you, I think she'd do far better to go to this audition and at least find out how she compares with the other girls, but she's had it so drummed into her during this last year how important it is to go on and finish her training that I'm afraid we're stuck with it for the time being."

"I'd be the last to try and talk her out of it, if that's what she's set on," I said, getting up, "but here's my telephone number, in case she changes her mind."

"Thanks a lot and I honestly do appreciate what you've tried to do. That's why I felt I owed it to you to let you in on the whole story, so you wouldn't think us ungrateful. It's funny about Lindy, you know; how people always do seem to rally round and lend a helping hand. She's bound to land on her feet, however high she jumps."

She accompanied me to the front door, but closed it behind me as soon as we had said goodbye and I had the feeling that she was deep in her armchair and her book again before I was back among the apples and tomatoes. I had been resigned to walking at least as far as the main road before finding a taxi, but in fact one drew up at the kerb as promptly as though it had been waiting in the wings. A girl got out and put two carrier bags down on the pavement while she paid the driver. She then turned and smiled briefly at me, before gathering up her load and walking away.

I did not believe it to be a smile of recognition and, although it was the second time we had come face to face, I might not have recognised her either, in any other surroundings. She had been so shy and demure, in her blue and white print dress, on that first occasion, bobbing her curtsey and murmuring her thanks with downcast eyes, as I handed her the silver cup. In the five days which had elapsed she seemed to have aged by as many years and she looked so confident, so lightfooted and so happy that she might have been Pippa passing.

I drove back to Beacon Square, feeling curiously uneasy and apprehensive.

TWENTY

(1)

"If it's any consolation to you," Robin said at dinner that evening, "Dexter isn't altogether satisfied with the verdict either. Not that he's ever been known to be completely satisfied about anything, one should add."

"How do you know he isn't?"

"He came to see me this afternoon. It was his day off. You wouldn't have thought so by the way he was spending it."

"What doesn't he like about the verdict?"

"He can't entirely accept the feasibility of swallowing sodium nitrate by mistake. If she'd been working in a lab, for instance, something of the kind could conceivably have occurred, but advanced science doesn't figure very prominently on the Waterside curriculum."

"Does that mean that he now veers to the suicide theory?"

"I gather not, since there hasn't been a shred of evidence that she ever threatened such a thing or was in any way neurotic."

"Apart from Vera's, of course."

"Which, as you'll recall, he was not privileged to hear."

"Did you tell him?"

"No, and I doubt if it would have made much difference. Probably Vera would now deny every word of it and, if she didn't, Dexter would discount most of what she said. He is inclined to distrust emotional women. You, on the other hand . . ."

"Me?"

"He seems to have been rather impressed by your evidence. He put you down as an observant and reliable witness."

"Good! Is he going to take it any further?"

"No, it's out of his hands now and he lacks the authority, in every sense, to press for a reopening of the case."

"So why did he come to see you?"

"Oh, that wasn't the only topic we discussed. We touched on a number of unrelated matters too, but I got the impression that he wanted to get this one off his chest before it was finally buried."

"He needs a good woman to confide in."

"Oh, undoubtedly."

We ate our dinner in silence for a while and then I said:

"Since we're going to Roakes this weekend, I might leave a bit early and take in Gillsford on the way. The trouble is that I'll need the car. Would you mind awfully coming down by train?"

"Not if it's that important to you. What is it this time? All part of the search for the good woman?"

"A good one and a bad one," I answered in suitably cryptic tones.

(2)

Tina had told me that the Blands always departed to their villa in France as soon as the school broke up for the summer, but since this had occurred ten days early, I hoped to find them still in residence at headquarters.

On the drive down from London I invented and rejected half a dozen explanations to account for my calling on them and by the time I turned into the Waterside drive had still not been able to hit on one which entirely satisfied me; or rather, which I could convince myself would have much chance of hoodwinking Connie Bland.

The only solution was to keep my fingers crossed that the moment would produce the inspiration and, in the meantime, I had another call to make first, over at The Lodge.

She looked older and more frail than ever, huddled in her armchair by the fireplace. An electric fire was burning in the grate and she had a rug over her knees, although the temperature in her little room already verged on the sweltering.

On top of the rug was a book, which she closed when I had knocked and been bidden to enter, and I saw that it was an old favourite by E. Nesbit. I could not swear that, for lack of a human audience, she had been reading aloud to the two dachshunds, but that was the impression I received, for they had both been sitting up on their haunches, looking very alert, but became supine as soon as I walked in, eyeing me inimically as though in disgust at the interruption of a much prized treat. Patsy's welcome fell short of the rapturous too:

"What? Back again?" she enquired in a voice which, by her standards, was noticeably sharp.

I hadn't bothered to invent any subtle excuses for this

visit and simply said I had heard she was not well and, being now on my way to Oxford, had taken the opportunity to stop and see how she was getting on.

"Not as well as I had hoped," she replied, still rather tetchy.

"You need a holiday."

"Oh, I know, that's what they all say. We'll see. I may go to my sister in Folkestone for a week or two later on. The trouble with her is, though, that she doesn't like dogs and I couldn't leave these two babies behind, could I now? It would be different if Pauline were going to be here. She'd look after them, I know. She loves taking them for walkies; but she'll be abroad with her parents."

"But there must be someone you could leave them with? I'm sure those jolly Spaniards would look after them like their own children."

"Everyone seems very anxious to get me away from here all of a sudden. Even you, Tessie."

"You can't blame us. You've had a rotten, worrying time and you need a change of scene."

"No, I don't. I have all the scene I need here, in my own cosy room, so stop beating about the bush and tell me what you've come for."

"Well, I've just done that, Patsy."

"Oh, you think I'm a silly old fool, don't you? You always have done, all you girls, and you may be right; but even I know that you don't have to go within miles of Gillsford to get from London to Oxford. So come on now! Out with it!"

"You're only half right," I told her. "I really did want to find out if you were feeling better and I'd probably have come anyway; but I admit there was something special I wanted to ask you."

"That's better! Fire ahead, then!"

"You remember telling me about your petty pilferer? The one who began by rifling the chocolate box and then moved on to bigger hauls?"

"I do indeed."

"You said you knew who was responsible and I thought you were referring to Hattie, but you weren't, were you?"

"Hattie? Good gracious, no. Whatever can I have said to give you that idea?"

"Well, for instance, that it wasn't worth stirring up a fuss because this girl would be leaving at the end of the term, which was certainly true of Hattie; and I already knew that she had this terrible addiction for sweets and suchlike."

"Oh, my dear child, that has nothing to do with it. Overeating is eating for eating's sake and kleptomania is stealing for stealing's sake. Didn't you know that?"

"I do now."

"If I'd left the box open on the table and invited Hattie to help herself, I've no doubt she'd have scoffed the lot, but taking them behind my back, without asking, oh dear me, no! I didn't always see eye to eye with poor Hattie, but to give her her due, she was as honest as the day. Besides, she had no need to take things which didn't belong to her. She could have bought up the lot of us with all the pocket money her father kept lavishing on her. Whereas . . ."

"Whereas Belinda Jameson was another kettle of fish? Belinda, who was also leaving at the end of the term, only in such unorthodox circumstances that I failed to make the connection."

"Yes, poor Lindy was quite a separate problem. She couldn't keep her hands off other people's property and she had a most dreadful obsession about money. She always wanted to be top dog, you see, poor child; to excel in everything and to be envied and admired by the others. Even her underclothes had to be smarter than theirs, although goodness knows what sacrifices her mother must have made to send her back with all that expensive, lacy stuff. It was so unnecessary too, because she would have excelled without any of that show. She was as clever as paint and a wonderful little actress. But there was just one thing she lacked and she ended by getting it out of all proportion."

"But you still didn't think of reporting her? It might have been better for her in the end, if you had, surely?"

"I couldn't say about that. Obviously, this weakness or whatever you like to call it had its origins in her father's crash, when she and her mother were reduced to dreadful poverty almost overnight. It happened at the very worst time, when Lindy was about thirteen. It's not surprising that it left some terrible scars. I tried to help her, build up her confidence and so on: I was always preaching that looks and brains and good health are what really count, but I can't claim to have made much impression."

"A psychiatrist might have had more success, don't you think?"

"Well, as to that, Tessie, I really couldn't say. I don't altogether hold with them, as you know. Sometimes I think they can do more harm than good and I've always believed that Lindy would grow out of this, once she was over the adolescent stage and no longer surrounded by these very rich girls, as most of them are. It was an artificial environment for her, you know. Being comparatively poor in the real world is very different from being a poor girl at Waterside."

"You saw an awful lot of what went on, didn't you, Patsy? How arrogant we were to . . ."

"Dismiss me as a silly old fuddy duddy, who couldn't see an inch in front of her nose? Well no, not really; I am a silly old fuddy duddy in lots of ways, and you girls are none the worse for it. Most of you have turned out fairly well, even though I did spoil you so dreadfully. And now, my child, are you going to stop for a cup of tea, or is it time to be moving on to your appointment in Oxford?"

"Yes, I ought to go, but I'll come and see you again."

"Yes, do, dear, and if you should happen to look in at headquarters before you leave, I wonder if you'd be kind enough to take this blouse for Mrs. Bland. I've been shortening the cuffs and I know she wants to take it to France with her, so she'd better try it on and make sure it's right."

Watching her as she folded the blouse and wrapped it in tissue paper, I wondered whether it was sheer fluke which had provided me with this errand, or whether shock and illness had so sharpened up Patsy's intuition that she had guessed that I needed some such excuse. On the other hand, the suspicion was dawning that she had always possessed such powers and that I had been the blinkered one, not to have recognised it. It was mortifying to discover how diametrically opposed everyone at Waterside was turning out to be to my childishly patronising view of them.

The interview with Connie provided few surprises, however, possibly because I was at last beginning to get her measure. She refused to answer any of my questions, saying that she had never heard such impudence in her life and I needn't imagine that just because I had always been rather a favourite it gave me the right to cross-examine her on matters which were no concern of mine. So I braced myself, drew a deep breath and gave her the answers myself. She heard me out, her snapping brown eyes fixed on me inscrutably, but she did not deny a single word and at the end spoke quite kindly, telling me to run along now, as she had important things to see to; also counselling me to work hard and not forget to eat occasionally.

So I drove into Gillsford and put my final question to Tina.

(3)

"It is another picture question," I told her. "And here is your starter for ten. Please cast your mind back to the art exhibition. I know you went on the opening day because I saw your name in the Visitors' Book, but can you remember exactly what time?"

"How can you expect me to be exact about a thing like that?" Tina asked with a horrible scowl.

"Be approximate then."

"Late afternoon . . . five-ish, five-thirty."

"After school tea, at any rate?"

"Yes."

"Which I remember as a rather festive occasion on Saturdays. Choccy bicks and so on; and, if anyone had had a birthday during the week, that was the day when the cake from home was ceremoniously cut and handed round. Is that custom still observed?"

"Yes."

"Good!"

"What's good about a lot of silly girls gorging themselves?"

"I'll tell you later. First, another question, and you can stop grimacing because we're nearly through now. Think carefully, please, Miss Blundell. When you visited the exhibition at five-ish or five-thirty, who was on reception duty?"

"No one. It wasn't necessary. All you official visitors had done your bit and the next lot weren't due till Sunday."

"Although we do know that Hattie went back later, either to collect something or because she couldn't bring herself to stay away. However, that's beside the point; so now cast your mind back for the last time. You are standing in the main gallery, so called, and facing you and dominating the whole scene is the portrait of Hattie's father. Remember?"

"Yes, perfectly."

"Right. And immediately to the left of it are a whole lot more of Hattie's pictures, including some rather dreary abstracts, as well as pen and ink drawings in the same style as the celebrated birds and fishes and my "Judgement Day" cartoon?"

"Yes."

"Among the latter, was there one of a masked girl in chains and an emaciated young man lying at her feet, apparently dead?"

"No."

"Quite sure? You've never seen it?"

"I'd have remembered if I had."

"And I believe you."

"However, since my evidence appears to be entirely negative, perhaps you'd explain why you're looking like the cat who swallowed the canary?"

"Well, you see, Tina, it was there earlier in the day and, more important still, it was there when the first visitors went round."

"How do you know it was?"

"Connie told me so herself. Or rather, I suggested that it might have been and she did not deny it, which amounts to the same thing. Apart from yourself, I cannot imagine a more reliable and observant witness."

"Oh, flattery now! And would you mind telling me what this new hare is that you're chasing?"

"No, when the time comes, I shan't mind at all. In fact, I shall positively enjoy it. And you were right, of course; you always are. You said all along that if one of Hattie's sketches revealed such dangerous knowledge that she was killed for it, then the murderer would have lost no time in destroying the sketch. How true that was! Actually, the picture may have been destroyed before the victim was dead, but that only proves you righter than ever."

"How you enjoy playing your little suspense games, don't you, Tessa? But, if you do mean to explain, I wish you'd get a move on."

"All in good time. I need a larger audience and, in the meantime, you and I have work to do."

"Work, she says! And me thinking the term has just ended and I could slacken off a bit!"

"This won't be very arduous. Billy Bland and I have a plan afoot to take you out of yourself."

"Very kind of you, but I prefer to stay inside myself."

"I know; that's your big trouble, but it's going to end. The wise old doctor considers there is too much work and not enough play in your life and he is relying on me to get the balance right. I have no intention of letting him down, so we shall now take the first step by tarting ourselves up to go out to dinner."

"Out to dinner where?"

"At Roakes Common. You haven't been there since you were fourteen years old, when Toby came over to fetch us out for lunch one Sunday. We spent the whole afternoon playing croquet and we never stopped quarrelling for a single minute, so it's high time to expunge that memory and show them all what sweet and civilised adults we've grown into."

"I must say I didn't realise what I was letting myself in for when I took you under my roof all those years later," Tina said.

"You don't know the half of it yet," I remarked, thinking of another little shock I had up my sleeve for her.

TWENTY-ONE

(1)

"It was Mrs. Jameson who started the ball rolling," I observed. "Gratifying how often it rebounds in one's favour when one sets out to do a good turn."

This was towards the end of dinner which, on that mid-summer evening, had been served on the flagged terrace at the back of Toby's house, by the light of candles and the setting sun.

The party was bowling along tolerably well, but there had been one major set-back, in the continuing absence of one of the guests. Having arranged to spend the weekend at Roakes, which was a frequent custom of ours throughout the year, I had asked if I might invite Tina for dinner on Saturday. This proving acceptable to our host, I had then suggested, as though as an afterthought, that we might as well try and cheer up poor lonely old Dexter by including him in the party. He too had accepted, although with certain reservations. He would be on duty until seven, so was almost bound to be late and on no account should we wait dinner for him.

This necessarily had an addling effect on a small plot I had been hatching, whereby Tina would make the journey to Roakes in his car, rather than mine. I still retained hopes of their doing the return trip together, but even these now looked in danger of being dashed on the rocks which Fate strews in our path, Robin having greeted us with the news that Dexter had telephoned only ten minutes earlier to say that he had been called out on an urgent case and was unable to estimate how long it might take him. He was therefore obliged to cancel the engagement altogether.

"What did you say?" I asked quickly.

"Oh, that he should try to make the effort to get over, however late, and we'd keep something hot for him. Knowing how keen you are to launch him into the social whirlpool, I told him that any time up to ten o'clock would be all right with us. I trust Tina won't mind, but I rather shoved the onus on to her."

"To me?" Tina demanded, sounding as though his trust had been misplaced.

"I'm afraid so. I told him we were depending on him for transport for one of the other guests. All nonsense, I need hardly say. Toby or I can easily run you back to Gillsford, but I couldn't think of anything which would induce Dexter to shuffle in on his own, halfway through dinner, except the belief that he would be letting someone else down by staying away."

"It seemed to me that I detected a note of over-earnestness in Robin's voice as he related all this, and also that he gave me the flicker of a wink, but unfortunately even such masterly tactics as he had deployed appeared to have failed and by half past nine our party was still incomplete. It was then that I threw out my remark about Mrs. Jameson.

"Where did she roll it to?" Toby enquired, getting up to refill our glasses.

"All over the place. She said that however high her Lindy jumped she would still land on her feet. Mind you, she had already come out with a number of illuminating remarks, but that one really set everything in place and as soon as I heard it I began to picture Belinda as a cat."

Robin and Toby looked quite as bemused as I had expected, but Tina said:

"The cat on the ladder?"

"Which led to something more. What do you associate with cats, apart from leaping about and landing on their feet?"

"Speaking for myself," Tina replied, "canaries, cream, mice and, of course, burglars."

"Right, as usual! I should explain here that when Patsy was telling me about the petty pilferer who operated so successfully at The Lodge, she mentioned that there had also been a genuine, professional break-in at headquarters and that cash and jewellery had been stolen from Connie's bedroom. She claimed there was no connection, but she was wrong. Belinda knew the Blands were spending the night in London and she really is as agile as a cat. She could easily have nipped up the front stairs and done the job in a couple of shakes, taking care, of course, to chuck a brick through the scullery window before she left. Patsy told me she was a girl who would risk anything for money and I believed it. In fact, I wouldn't mind betting it was she who pinched five or six pounds out of my coat pocket one sunny morning. She was clever about covering her tracks too. She let Patsy believe that her mother paid for all the expensive finery she brought back to school and she told her mother it was given to her by the other girls, because she was so popular."

"And all the time buying it with stolen money?" Toby asked. "Well, I never did!"

"It needn't do you for long," I said, "because that's not how it was. Much more likely that she acquired most of it by shoplifting."

Tina said reprovingly: "Oh, come on now, don't exaggerate. You've made out a reasonable enough case, so far, and it's no special news to me, I might add, but you don't need to throw in shoplifting as well."

"How about this, then? According to Mrs. Jameson, who obviously has no idea what her pretty angel gets up to, the only way which occurs to Belinda to earn some money during the holidays is to get taken on by the big stores in their summer sales. Now, I ask you. What more ideal hunting ground for a light-fingered little girl, who also happens to be as sharp as a needle?"

At this point Robin, who is mad for brass tacks, interrupted by asking:

"And does all this lead up to your telling us that Hattie had discovered all these crimes and that Belinda killed her, to prevent the news from spreading?"

"That did occur to me," I admitted, "but I soon realised that it wouldn't do. You see, the news already had spread to the only quarter where it really mattered. I must now explain that Connie had been keeping Belinda on at school absolutely free of charge, because she was so promising and so likely, ultimately, to reflect credit on the school. So it was a gamble, in a sense; but, having backed her fancy, Connie didn't sit back and let the horse do the rest. She kept a strict and vigilant eye on Belinda and towards the end it was becoming painfully clear to her that things were getting into a pickle. So when she came back from London to find that thieves had gone straight to her bedroom, taken cash and jewellery, but completely ignored all the valuable objects with which that part of the house is stuffed, it didn't take her long to identify the culprit."

"You honestly believe Connie knew?" Tina asked, sounding startled for once.

"She as good as told me so. That's to say, I put it to her and she didn't so much as blink. I also suggested that she had hauled Belinda up for a stewards' enquiry, if you'll forgive my continuing with the racing metaphor, and issued an ultimatum."

"Warned her off, I suppose you mean?" Toby said.

"Yes, in other words, told Belinda that she would not be allowed to stay at Waterside after the end of the term, but could remain till then and take part in the drama competition. Furthermore, not a word would be passed on to the police, or Belinda's mother, or anyone at all, provided she behaved herself. The promise was most readily given, needless to say, but of course the news travelled that she'd got the push and since, ostensibly, there was no crime to account for it, everyone assumed that it was because her mother couldn't afford the fees, which is rather ironical, when you think of it."

"So why did Connie change her mind and break the agreement?" Tina asked.

"On the contrary, she didn't break the agreement, it was Belinda who did that. She really is a worry, that girl. She raided the till just after all the big spenders had been into the shop on Saturday morning. Connie caught her in the act and fired her on the spot. For once in her life, she acted on impulse and you really can't blame her. She'd had a rotten time, one way and another, and this was the last straw. As we know, she relented later and Belinda survived to kick another leg, but that was because a far worse catastrophe had occurred, which put everything else in the shade. However, that's not quite the end of Belinda; she still has a walk-on part in the last act."

"Quite a character!" Toby remarked. "And only sixteen, you say? She must have a great future."

"Mostly in Holloway, by the sound of it."

"Oh, don't say that, Robin. I really hope she does manage to keep out of trouble in future; and, if so, she's going to be really good news in the theatre."

"What happens in the last act?" Tina asked.

"It opens with the big question," I replied. "How did Hattie get to hear about the burglary and how did she know Belinda was the thief? Clearly, she was expert at ferreting out information, and she was also given the run of the place, but she can hardly have been a witness to this particular episode. Furthermore, we've all had firsthand experience of Connie's ability to clamp down on bad news and she'd given Belinda her word that it wouldn't go any further. Even Patsy never knew who was responsible. But I put it to Connie that she must have talked things over with Billy before coming to a decision and she didn't deny that either. It wasn't necessary to ask whether Pauline was present during the discussion, because either she was, or she overheard it. It has to be one or the other."

"Why does it?" Tina asked.

"Because there's simply no other way that Hattie could

have got to hear about it. And you know so well that it's exactly the kind of thing Pauline would do. Even in our day she was always running back and forth with bits of news and gossip and trying to curry favour by letting us into little secrets. But the one she would have wanted to curry favour with most of all was Hattie."

"Why?"

"Do you remember telling me that Pauline was one of the few people who had any time for Hattie? Well, you were right, as usual and it probably began with those taxi rides to Oxford. They took place twice a week regularly for almost a year and in those circumstances you could hardly avoid getting to know your fellow passenger as an individual, although the chances are that Pauline gave out a lot more about her own aspirations and hang-ups than Hattie ever did. But the significant thing is that when I mentioned it to Pauline she flatly denied that they had ever been on any sort of personal footing. Whereas one would have expected her to be quite boastful about it."

"Why would one?" Tina asked.

I was getting annoyed by these incessant "whys" with which she found it necessary to punctuate practically every statement and I said:

"Oh, use your loaf, or your feet, or something. You know very well Pauline would have basked in the reputation of being Hattie's special crony. She was Connie's prize pet, who could do no wrong and any friend of hers would have won great approval, the one thing Pauline longed for and never achieved. You have to hand it to old Connie, incidentally. She may be a snob and a money worshipper, but she worships talent even more. Hence her generosity to Belinda, for which she got no thanks from anyone. However, you put me off with your constant interruptions and now I'm digressing. Where had I got to?"

"You were telling us," Robin said, "how Pauline had denied having any dealings with Hattie on a personal level."

"Yes, and she was most positive about it too, which suggested to me that she was probably lying, so I asked myself why, came up with a possible answer and after that there was nothing much to it. Just a question of collating all the known facts and getting confirmation of a few others, as yet unproven, and there we were."

"Where?" Tina began, but this time I was ready for her:

"I refer, as you'll have gathered, to the business of establishing beyond reasonable doubt that Pauline murdered Hattie."

"Okay, go ahead and establish it," she advised me.

"I have a feeling that was the intention anyway," Toby informed her. There was a hint in his tone that he did not find Tina's company the most congenial in the world, but since I had no ambition to marry them off this did not bother me.

"Do you remember, I asked him, "my telling you and Robin that one of the few sensational events in my Waterside career was when Pauline was carted off by ambulance in the middle of the night? We were told she had acute appendicitis, but we all assumed automatically that she had tried to commit suicide. You must remember it too, Teeny? It was soon after she was eased out of that job with her father's practice, which she made such a botch of and where also, I should remind you, she had complete access to his dispensary. And thereby hangs another tale, which I'll come to in a moment. Meanwhile, we now jump forward again to the time when Hattie and Pauline are making their twice-weekly trips to Oxford, a momentous period for Pauline because for the first time in her life she has broken loose from some of her chains and has the freedom to follow her own devices. Inevitably, alas, they lead her into trouble and she goes completely overboard for the first young man ever to show any interest in her, oblivious until too late that he has simply been using her and that he happens to be a confirmed drug-addict. Inevitably too, in my opinion, before the shattering disillusionment came, she would have confided in Hattie that she was in love and soon to be married, with a dear little home of her own. We can be sure that Hattie lent a sympathetic ear, which is why it must have seemed such a terrible betrayal when, two years later, Pauline accompanied her parents round the art exhibition and saw Hattie's cruel picture. It was my guess that it was this which drove her to homicidal insanity, quite as much as the fear that her earlier crime was about to be resurrected, after believing that after all this time it was safely buried."

Robin and Toby accepted this pronouncement with puzzled, attentive expressions, but Tina, never at a loss, said in a superior voice:

"Honestly, Tessa, all this conjecture! Are you making it up as you go along, by any chance?"

"No, not at all, it's the only logical explanation. You see, the picture I refer to," I went on, turning to the more docile members of my audience, "portrayed a young woman, masked and bound in chains, with a dead man lying at her feet."

"From which you deduce that Pauline had killed him?" Robin asked. "Then I think I'm on Tina's side this time. Unless you have left out quite a lot, that does seem to have been quite a jump. I can see how you might associate chains with Pauline, but since the female figure was masked . . ."

"You have every right to be sceptical," I said, "since neither of you was educated at Waterside, but Tina knows the background as well as I do. Hattie went in for rather lurid but nevertheless apposite titles and this particular one was called 'Perils of Revenge'. Now, although the first word in that title might not lead you two straight to Pauline, it would certainly have done so for anyone grounded as we all were in the history and classics of the cinema. The picture disappeared, so far as we have been able to narrow it down, between four o'clock and five-thirty on Saturday afternoon, Hattie having been temporarily lured away by the prospect of a whacking great tea at The Lodge. To be greeted on her return, no doubt, by Pauline with her little bottle of infallible slimming pills. Whereupon, Hattie, in a temporary mood of remorse for having tucked in so lavishly to the cake and chocolate biscuits, cheerfully swallows the dose as prescribed by Pauline. To conclude: the other thing that Tina knows is that approximately two years ago a young man in Oxford, known to be a drug addict, died after taking sodium nitrate. That's not conjecture, it's a fact, isn't it, Tina?"

She continued to scowl at me in a fairly frightening way, but for the first time nodded in assent and Robin asked:

"And did Mrs. Bland admit, or fail to deny, that Pauline had once tried to kill herself with sodium nitrate and might, unknown to anyone, have kept a little stock of it hidden away for emergencies?"

"No, I confess I had already gone as far as I dared by then; slightly further, in fact."

"So unless Pauline confesses, and I really don't see why she should, none of this can be proved?"

"No."

"So may one ask what you propose to do?" Tina asked, rallying again.

"Nothing. It's not in my power to do anything. As you say, I can't prove it, but so far as I'm concerned it's the only explanation which covers everything and I thought it might amuse you to hear how I reached it."

"And it sounds as though telling us will be enough for you," Toby said. "I do hope so. There appears to be enough unpleasantness already."

There was still a little more to come, however, for while he was speaking the telephone could be heard ringing in the hall and he went on, without a pause:

"Mrs. Parkes will have retired by now, so one of you had better answer that."

Unfamiliar with his dementia about telephone callers, Tina looked faintly startled when Robin got up without a word and went indoors. Then, returning her attention to me, she said:

"You claim that you don't intend to do anything about it, but would you have told us all this if the Sergeant had been here?"

"You've got me there," I confessed, "and this time I'm stumped for the answer."

"But you must have known whether you intended to or not, when we set out this evening?"

"Not really. I had it in mind to tell Robin and Toby because I never can resist that; you too, eventually, but I'm not perfectly sure whether that would have been the end of it or not."

"Perhaps you'd have been afraid that an expert would have found all sorts of flaws which you'd overlooked?"

"No, certainly not, I . . ."

"Why don't you stay the night, Tina?" Toby suggested. "Then you and Tessa can thrash it all out in the morning over a jolly game of croquet?"

"Oh yes, do, Tina, that's a marvellous idea! Toby has a whole cupboardful of spare toothbrushes, so you've no excuse at all."

"Robin came out of the house, saying: "That was Dexter. Very sorry, but he can't make it. This case he was called out on took him longer than he expected."

"Oh, what a blow!"

"I suggested he might come over for lunch tomorrow instead," Robin said, looking round the table. "I knew Toby wouldn't mind."

"Oh, lovely! And Tina's staying the night, so it'll be mallets for five!"

"I haven't said . . ." Tina began.

"No, but you will, won't you? We all want you to. By the way, Robin," I went on quickly, to deter her from further argument, "what was the case that delayed him so badly? Did he tell you?"

"Yes, and rather a curious coincidence, in view of our conversation just now," he replied, addressing Tina. "Another fatality at Waterside, I regret to say."

Since she refrained from asking the obvious question, I did so for her.

"Pauline," he answered.

"No? Honestly? Not another . . . ?"

"No, not murder, or anything of that kind. In fact, she appears to have died rather heroically."

"What happened?"

"She was drowned, apparently in an attempt to save the life of a dachshund, who'd jumped or fallen in the river.

It seems it was quite old and going a bit blind. They found its brother whimpering on the bank. Pauline couldn't swim very well and, although you can't see them on the surface, there are masses of weeds where she went in. She got badly tangled up."

"For the last, but not the only time," I remarked, avoiding Tina's glare.

(2)

"It's been a real old bag of mixed blessings this time," I confessed when Robin and I were alone at last. "And in some ways I'm sorry they ever invited me to be a judge. I've learnt too many things I'd rather not have known. And to think I spent all those years looking back on Waterside as such a placid, well-ordered place, where the most exciting thing that could happen was for someone to be accepted by the Royal Ballet School."

"Don't be sad," he replied. "Things will soon get back to normal. Your indomitable ex-principal is not one to be put down for long by a few setbacks of this nature."

"Oh, I'm not worried about Connie," I assured him. "She has no maternal instinct, or if she has it is all reserved for her richest and most talented pupils. She certainly had very little to spare for Pauline and it would never surprise me if she had said the word to wipe that particular slate clean. She may not have found it prudent to mention this to Sergeant Dexter, but the fact is that Pauline was a very good swimmer. It was one of the few things she did well. But in any case Connie despised failures and I doubt if the memory of a failure is any harder to live with than the reality."

"So is it Belinda you're worried about?"

"Not specially. As Patsy so shrewdly remarked, Waterside was such an artificial environment and she probably has a good chance of straightening herself out when she's competing on what she regards as equal terms."

"What is the trouble then?"

"Oh, Eddie, mainly."

"Eddie? But I understood that he and Vera were now completely in the clear?"

"Oh, as to Vera, I wouldn't like to say. I admit she had nothing to do with the murder, but every one of Hattie's pictures told a story, and most of them turned out to be true. It wouldn't surprise me if she'd got this one right, as well, and that was why Vera came ricocheting out of the art exhibition as one pursued by a bear. Not that I care a damn about her; it's Eddie who's the worry. I dare say Toby was joking, but ever since he came up with that idea of Eddie being a spy I've been stuck with it. I've always thought he was rather an ass, but such a dear too, and now I know I'll never feel easy with him again."

"Just supposing there really were some truth in it, there are spies and spies, you know, Tessa."

"You mean . . . commercial . . . industrial . . . that kind of thing?"

"No, not that kind of thing at all. Try again!"

I did so and came up beaming:

"Oh yes, I see! You mean, Eddie is on our side? He's working for us?"

"I shouldn't think so for a moment, but why not ask him?"

"Oh, what's the use of that? If I said to him: 'By the way, Eddie, are you a spy?' he'd be sure to say 'Yes', and I still shouldn't know whether to believe him. How frustrating!"

"Well, stop feeling frustrated because we end on a happier note. I have two cheering items of news for you. That is, if I can stay awake long enough to pass them on."

"Make a stern effort, please, because good news has been in rather short supply lately. What are they?"

"The first is that Belinda didn't steal the money from your pocket."

"She didn't? How do you know?"

"As a matter of fact, I stole it myself."

"Robin! Out of my pocket?"

"No, you'd put it in the glove compartment of the car.

I thought that was a silly place to leave cash lying around, so I took it out and then forgot to give it to you. I'm so sorry. I did mean to tell you, but it went clean out of my head."

"Oh, I don't mind a bit. I'm just so thankful that we can cross Belinda's name off that one. I can't tell you how glad I am; and also that I awarded her top marks in the competition. What's the other news?"

"Your agent telephoned."

"Oh yes? What did she want?"

"She wanted to know where the hell you'd been all day and why she hadn't been able to get in touch with you."

"Come on, Robin, don't tease! What did she really want?"

"Now, let me think. Ah yes, I remember. It was just to say that you've got the part."

"I've . . . got . . . what?"

"You heard!"

"I've actually got it? You really mean that?"

"Every word."

"Oh, but this is wonderful! I can't believe it! I've never been more happy or more terrified in my whole life. Now perhaps we'll be able to afford a second car? One thing I know for certain, though: I'm going to make a success of this, if it's the last thing I ever do. From now on, I shall devote myself exclusively to work, heart and soul and twenty-four hours a day. I'll never again get mixed up in other people's lives or their deaths either; and this time I do mean it. Are you listening, Robin?"

But he was already half asleep. He had heard it all before.

CATHERINE AIRD

For 15 years, Catherine Aird's mysteries have won praises for their brilliant plotting and style. Established alongside other successful English mystery ladies, she continues to thrill old and new mystery fans alike.

The Deadly Arts

Tessa Crichton, actress wife of Scotland Yard Inspector
Robin Price, takes a break from trodding the boards to
visit her old alma mater...and ends up playing the part
of sleuth. The girls at Waterside Drama and Ballet
School are all very talented. But one of them excels at
snooping into other people's secrets...and learns too
late that a little knowledge can be a most dangerous
thing. Something that nosey seventeen-year-old Hattie
McGrath found out was lethal enough to get her killed.
Was it illicit love among the staff? Stealing among the
students? Espionage among the alums? Or a scheme so
beastly that Tessa's search for a killer becomes an education in the elusive evil one might find behind the
most friendly facade.

A Tessa Crichton Mystery

25647

0

76783 00295

N 0-553-25647-5>>295

W8-CAN-222